Faithless Elector
By James McCrone

For Lisa

I am deeply grateful to the following people during the preparation of this book for their support, diligence, insight, attention to detail and good sense: Jim McCue, editor; my family—Lisa, Fiona, Annie and Jake, Don & Carole, Elmer & Lois; Michele Mendelssohn
To all of them, thank you.

"I see my opportunity and I take it."
George Washington Plunkitt, Tammany Hall

ELECTION NIGHT

November 9th, 2016: Wichita 3:54 a.m.

Five televisions, each tuned to different channels painted the penthouse suite at the Ambassador Hotel in flickering light, the shifts on the screens reflecting in the eyes of three men anxiously watching. As the votes of one state after another came in, each man would glance furtively over his shoulder toward the nearest bedroom, its door open, darkened as though no one were in it.

"It's been a dead heat," said one of the anchors. "The Electoral College vote and the popular vote were both evenly split between Redmond and Christopher all the way to the Pacific Coast Time Zone."

"The polls have been closed in Illinois for seven hours now," said another anchor. "Right now James Christopher leads, but if Illinois' twenty Electoral College votes go to Diane Redmond, she will win by four votes. If Illinois goes to Christopher, then he wins by a full forty-seven votes. This could be a squeaker, like the 2000 election. I wonder if anyone is asleep tonight."

Just after four in the morning, Central Standard Time, the final network announced a winner: "With the last precincts reporting, we can now say that Diane Redmond has been elected the first female president of the United States, with a presumed Electoral College Vote of 267 to 271. The margin of victory is just four—that's one electoral vote less than those separating Bush and Gore in 2000, when Bush won the Electoral College vote, but Gore won the popular vote."

The only one of the three men on the couch who hadn't yet poured himself a fresh drink now stood up to do so; and as he did, he muted the final television. Exhausted, backs to the screens, the three men leaned on the bar, staring at anything but one another. None hazarded a glance toward the darkened bedroom.

Finally, one of the men went over to the gaggle of remotes by the couch and ceremoniously turned off the televisions, as in an earlier, simpler time, he might have put out the candles before retiring to bed.

"Well," said the man holding the remotes, "that's it. It's over."

"The hell it is," said a voice from the threshold of the bedroom.

CHAPTER ONE

November 11, 2016: Seattle

Matthew Yamashita stood in his graduate advisor's office, papers spread across a table at one side of the room.

"Looks good," said his advisor, Duncan Calder, looking over Matthew's surveys. "Everyone signed up?"

"Yeah, we'll begin on Monday. One thousand seventy-six telephone surveys. Each student has nine electors to call. I gave a few of them who are specially keen a couple more. I just…"

"You're worried."

"Duncan, I'm freaking out."

Calder smiled kindly. "You've worked and reworked the survey. It's sound. Be proud of that." Calder considered putting a comforting hand on Matthew's shoulder but decided against it.

Professor Duncan Calder was 47 and handsome, with strong, black Irish features and a penetrating gaze. His hazel-green eyes could look either menacing or warm, a facility he used to great effect with undergrads and grad students alike, keeping them guessing endlessly whether he liked them particularly, liked everyone in general or was a selfish, self-absorbed son of a bitch. Matthew was special in Calder's eyes.

"More than that, Matthew," continued Calder, "by using the class as your polling organization you are giving undergrads a hands-on look at how polls are conducted. It's a unique opportunity for them. I'll make sure they know it.

"Listen, I often tell grad students not to forget that no one knows as much about their topic as they do. But Matthew, not only do you know more about this than anyone else, you are the first I am aware of to track Electors nationally. You're the only one amassing data on who the Electoral College voters are."

November 12, 2016 Lewiston, Maine

A group of volunteer firemen looked at each other in astonishment as their truck rounded the last bend in the lane before what was left of the farmhouse. The neighbor who had called them ran toward the truck as it ground to a halt. Black smoke poured past the truck's headlights. As they unloaded hoses, the neighbor called out: "He must still be in there!" Silently, the firemen set about the only thing they could do: contain the fire.

"This is his car," she repeated in horror. "He's still in there." The captain looked at what was left of the blazing house and shook his head at her, but not because he didn't believe her. She drew her heavy coat about her tightly and shivered, though within the ring of light created by the burning house it was warm.

November 12, 2016 Bedford, Massachusetts

Traffic traveling west or east on Route 3, slowed to a crawl as cars were waived around the bend in single file. Ten cars drove west, then ten east, past the squad cars and slowly dying road flares. But there was no more to see. The dead man lay forty yards past the edge of the road.

"Drunk probably," said the state patrolman to the man and woman from the coroner's office who arrived to take the body. "Barely any skid," he added, pointing back toward deputies diligently measuring and photographing every inch of asphalt up to the crest of the bend from which the dead man had launched himself.

"Nice bike ... was," said the first reporter on the scene as the dead man's new looking Harley-Davidson was illuminated by a camera flash. In the red and blue strobe half-light, the workers from the coroner's office stood back from the county photographer, arms folded across their chests, each bearing an expression of frustrated impatience. "Can we get on with it now?" the woman asked. "Cold out here," the man added. "Let's get this drunk under wraps."

November 13, 2016 Iowa City, Iowa
The garbage truck driver had been the first to notice the young widow in the snow behind her large house. Clearly she had slipped on the ice leading to the back gate while taking the garbage out the night before. Light snow had covered her tracks, but the shopping bag full of trash lay in front of her, covered in the same powdery veil.

"Least I can do is take her garbage for her," he said to the policeman, who looked at his sergeant, who looked at the detective, who nodded that it was OK. All that day and the next, at odd moments, the sight of her—pale even against the fresh snow, eyes open—floated to the surface of his thoughts; the image of lightly crystalline frost running from the bottom of her nose, past her chin to her throat and lingering in her ear, reminded him of the furry mold that often covered the fruit and vegetables he saw during the summer.

November 14, 2016: Yamhill, Oregon
After days of neither seeing the old truck come or go, a neighbor had come to see if anything was wrong. Now, the police had arrived, too. On a hillside overlooking Oregon's Willamette Valley, Don Meadows had been perfecting a *méthode champenoise* blend from his own Chardonnay and Pinot Noir grapes, which he had claimed would rival anything from France.

As he stood in the "cave," a converted barn, turning

—

bottles to move the sediment toward the neck, one had exploded. A shard containing the imprint of the bottle's punt was lodged in the side of his neck, having severed the carotid artery. The leather apron with neck guard that his daughter had bought him for this hazardous routine hung quietly on a peg.

"You know," said the neighbor to the sheriff, "he's lucky. His daughter'd've kill him if she'd found he wasn't wearing that apron."

November 18, 2016, 6:10 a.m. Washington, DC
In her basement office of FBI Public Corruption Unit along Pennsylvania Avenue, agent Imogen Trager, paused before hitting "send".

Her note to her boss, the Executive Assistant Director, Doug Pollack, read: RE: Illinois/ USAO request.

Doug, I have looked at the small sampling of election results I was able to obtain in connection with the USAO's request that we look into whether the anonymous tampering allegations have any merit. The sampling I have from the Illinois election results is inconclusive. There may indeed be tampering, but I can't yet say one way or the other.

To do a full analysis I will need a much bigger data sample. Let me know how you would like me to proceed.

CHAPTER TWO

December 5, 2016: Seattle

In a Montlake basement apartment, Matthew Yamashita's eyes started open. His heart beat frantically. He looked at the alarm clock: 8:30 a.m. Lecture beginning in an hour.

He rushed around the darkened bedroom, pausing in his frenzy to get dressed only long enough to smell each article of clothing he picked up from the floor before putting it on. His medium length jet-black hair stood improbably straight as it rose away from his sleep-creased face. Minor hair flips and explosive tufts created a lumpy, elephantiasis effect at the sides and back of his head.

Matthew frowned as he smelled his socks, but put them on anyway. He pulled up his long johns, taking care the socks stayed tucked underneath the cuffs, then pulled on a faded pair of baggy jeans, the belt still in the loops. Cinching the belt tight across his narrow waist, he struggled into a pale green T-shirt, which he tucked absently into the front. Next, a pale blue oxford cloth shirt. He bothered only with the bottom four buttons. Once dressed, he filled the sink with warm water and plunged his head into it. He toweled off quickly. As he patted the dark bags under his eyes with the towel, he wondered how he could look so tired when he had slept so long.

Out of habit, he opened the refrigerator, perhaps hoping that something had appeared overnight. But the molding bread, damp inside its bag, the yellowed celery, and the cellophane bag bulging with brown water that had once been spinach were still all that was available. He slammed the door in disgust.

He began collecting his books and papers and stuffing

them in his backpack. As he picked up the papers he had worked on the night before, he tore a strip of paper from a pile on his desk, turned it over to make sure nothing important was written on it, and then scribbled on the back: "Dead Electors—alternates?" He stuffed the paper into the breast pocket of his shirt and grabbed his jacket.

Head down, pedaling his 12-speed for all it was worth, he tore up Rainier Vista, a broad gravel path leading into the heart of the UW campus. As his legs pumped, he could feel himself sweating inside his Gortex jacket, his body producing a dank, humid dew that pasted his shirt to his back. At Drumheller Fountain he veered left and dropped the bicycle to a lower gear.

He jumped off and slotted the machine into the bike rack outside of Johnson Hall. He had two minutes before he would be late. Professor Calder began his lectures on time, and he expected his teaching assistants to be prompt as well, whatever their other duties or problems.

The slightly rusted bicycle lock clasp took three minutes of romancing before it would open. Matthew looked at his watch, cursed under his breath and took the stairs at a dead run.

Calder was just beginning as Matthew walked calmly into the lecture hall for Political Science 202, Introduction to American Politics. Professor Calder looked directly at Matthew and then looked back at his notes, as though suddenly very tired.

Matthew's surveys were going forward, but not well. Using unpaid students as his polling organization had been fraught with setbacks. Matthew had not anticipated the level of direction, coaching and supervision the students would need. At times when they were working he had felt like he was proctoring an exam, as he strode through the rows of them seated at tables.

"You shouldn't be eating while talking on the phone," he

had had to say to one; "You can't ask them to wait while you take a personal call!" he had almost shouted at another.

And while he had allowed for a number of no-shows, he had not foreseen the lack of commitment with which he was confronted. He had been forced to do more of the work himself, and to push more of it than he had planned onto the pair of work-study students for whom he had grant money. All of it had extended the data collection time, and Calder was not pleased.

Before Matthew had all his papers and notebooks in order, Calder had begun, pacing slowly back and forth behind the lectern. "I'd like to discuss the Electoral College system for electing the president today, first approaching it historically, and then moving into a discussion which will focus on aspects I hope will speak directly to some of the work you've been doing with Mr. Yamashita." As he said this, Calder quit his slow pace back and forth behind the podium and came to rest next to it. He shot a meaningful glance at Matthew. Matthew assumed the look meant, "You had better be ready."

"As you know," Calder continued, "this is a system by which the president is not chosen directly, but by Electors in each state..."

As Calder spoke, Matthew began ruminating on his surveys. It had all taken much longer than he had anticipated. And now, as he was finally getting to the end, his work-study students were having to go back to the state parties and get alternate names for deceased Electors in Maine, Massachusetts, Iowa and some other states. He knew, or hoped he knew, that both work-study students were already on the job, and he burned to be there with them to help finish the collection and finalize coding the protocols.

"Professor Calder," a young student asked, breaking Matthew's concentration, "I've been hearing on the news that the Illinois results may be wrong. That there was tampering.

—

9

Are they hiding something?"

"I'm not sure who 'they' are."

"The government, the Democrats."

"I would be careful of looking too quickly for conspiracies." Professor Calder flashed a meaningful look in Matthew's direction. "As you recall," he began, returning his address to the class at large, "the difference between the vote was very close in Illinois, and Christopher originally held off conceding until there had been a recount."

Calder paused and looked about the lecture hall. "The Illinois election officials ordered a recount. Now, I'm pretty sure that, more than a reaction to Christopher's claims, the recount was merely standard procedure when the outcome is so close. Many states have such requirements. And at any rate, the recount was conducted and the result has stood. Christopher has conceded."

"Then why is it still all over the news?" the student began.

"I think you will find that most news organizations have moved on, and that only one network is beating the drum about this."

"So there's absolutely nothing to these reports?" she asked.

"Well," said Calder, "if there were tampering, it was clearly not of an obvious kind, like when the vote for one candidate exceeds the number of registered voters in the precinct, or an auditor notices that the voters for a particular candidate showed up at the polls in alphabetical order." Calder paused and smiled.

"It has also happened in some elections," he continued, "that the dead were so moved by affairs of this world that they rose and cast their votes with remarkable unanimity for one particular candidate. All these kinds of fraud are obvious and easily uncovered, and none of it happened in Illinois. The Illinois election office and the Illinois Attorney General are satisfied with the result, which is the end of it."

Calder felt he had put an end to this line of questioning, but he worried that he was letting an opportunity slip by. "Having said that, there are subtle ways of engineering an outcome. I'm not saying for a moment this is what happened, but maybe if I walked you through a scenario of how you might tamper with a result you would see why, even though nothing obvious has turned up, there is always room for doubt, and why that doubt serves to make headlines and sell newspapers because it is difficult to prove conclusively one way or another."

Calder noticed that a number of students sat up straighter.

"First," Calder began, "this kind of thing has been going on as long as there have been elections. Everyone knows how to do it, and each side knows that the other side knows how to do it, so they will be watching for it. You have to be careful. Do nothing that would invite attention or scrutiny-- something no one wants when they are breaking the law." He paused and there was general, scattered nodding from the students. "Minimize your exposure."

"So, across the country, there are districts and precincts that are called 'safe' for one party; that is, a candidate for the other party doesn't stand a chance at the full election. This state of affairs does not in itself breed political corruption because, really, why would you bother? *But*, when a state is made up of many 'safe' districts—some Democrat and some Republican—it can get interesting, because at state-wide and national elections, those various safe districts are competing against one another for their party's candidates. It's winner-take-all for presidential and senatorial elections, so the stakes are very high.

"Within each safe district, the dominant party will have their people doing all the major and minor tasks: from election officials to poll workers, even poll watchers. That

---

11

situation is called having 'control'. Your party-loyal workers at the polls will be keeping track of who has voted and who has not. Meanwhile, your people are counting the ballots cast in that precinct. As other precincts start releasing their numbers you wait to release yours and watch how the results are going statewide.

"Instead of blatantly stuffing the ballot box, you prepare extra, bogus votes for people who are registered, but have not voted." He mimed a box under his left arm, from which the bogus votes would come, "and as you tally the results from a precinct over which your party has control, you start looking carefully at the reports from other precincts--ones that have historically had majorities for candidates of the other party. If you see that you are ahead, you do nothing—you've won fair and square; but if you are behind a precinct that has already reported its results, then you wait and report with just enough extra votes to tip the statewide balance in your favor. The advantage, therefore, if you are attempting to engineer an outcome, is to report last, because you will have more information.

"If you see that you need some votes," he held up his mimed box and began walking in front of the first row, handing out votes. "But if you don't need the votes," Calder mimed placing the box behind him, and held out both of his hands, showing there was nothing in them: "you do nothing. Why draw attention to yourself for no reason?

"And let's be honest here—it is rare that only one side is doing this sort of engineering, so on your side you have to wait for the other side to commit. Back to my original point: since everyone involved knows how this kind of thing works and both sides may be doing it, when there is a discernible pattern of late returns, red flags go up.

"In Illinois, some have alleged that there seems to have been a pattern of late returns, which could mean tampering, but it would take a thorough and exhaustive interrogation of the facts. And, further, the reasons that it will be further difficult to prove, if indeed such a scenario has happened, speak directly to what we have been concerning ourselves with in this class for the past few weeks--the influence of political parties and the loyalty they may or may not command; and because those doing the engineering will have sought to minimize their profile, only a few people--the smallest possible number--will have direct knowledge of the tampering. And it will be in their best interest to hang together, lest they hang separately."

Professor Calder paused. "I've been making light of this somewhat, but I know it's also serious. If they suspected there had been fraud, they would have to look not only at this election, but at past elections; and if the reporting differed from voting patterns established by prior elections, they would have circumstantial evidence upon which to investigate further.

"Circumstantial evidence, please remember, is not as bad as courtroom dramas make it out to be. If you wake up tomorrow morning and there is snow on the ground, you may assume that it snowed while you were asleep. But without an eyewitness to the snow having actually fallen, you will be basing your assumption on circumstantial evidence."

Calder looked at the clock, noticing he was nearly out of time. He paused and smiled. "I'd like to leave you with one last point on this score," he said, "and it is from Thoreau: 'Some circumstantial evidence is persuasive,' he said. 'If you find trout swimming in your delivered milk, you may be sure they are watering the milk'."

Matthew was one of the first out the lecture hall when Professor Calder had finished his reminder of the reading due for the following lecture.

He rode quickly over to the basement rooms he had been assigned for his survey center in the student union building. Both his students were at work.

"OK, where are we?" he asked as he strode into the room, throwing his book bag on one chair and his jacket onto another.

"Gettin' there," said the more communicative of the two.

Matthew grabbed the nearest pile of surveys. Each field on the survey was assigned a numeric value. The first field showed the level of contact and was assigned a number: "1" meant the interview had been completed; "2" meant it had been started but not completed; and "3" meant No Response.

Matthew rifled through the first stack and then the second, seeing "1" at the top of each protocol. "Great," he said, "great. Full contact."

"I suppose we should code all these dead ones as threes, for No Response, right?"

"I guess so," said Matthew. "This has been bugging me since I read your email. How many dead Electors do you have?"

The student shrugged without looking up. Although the work-study student was intelligent, his absolute lack of social grace or interpersonal skill belied his abilities. He never looked anyone in the eye, but rather cast a peripatetic gaze so quickly it made his body sway slightly on the rare occasions that he spoke. He was large, pimpled and sweated to excess. The exertion of merely sitting caused him to wheeze and huff as though he had run a long distance.

"In most of the cases, we've got the alternate anyway," said the student.

"Good," said Matthew. "But how many?"

"Five," said the student.

"Five of the people we tried to contact are dead?"

"Seven," said the other student, sitting across the table from the first one. He handed Matthew the phone sheet he had just finished working on. "Five from him and two from me."

"That's weird. Seven people?"

14

"People die," the first student shrugged. "Seven out of 300 million people is not weird." He stuffed a chocolate bar into his mouth.

"Yeah," Matthew shrugged and went back to his own work. He put the dead Elector surveys aside in one pile and began coding the others into his computer.

"I'm pretty much done," said the pimpled one.

"OK," said Matthew, "start by filling in as much as you can for the dead ones and then continue with this second pile, while I work on the first. We'll merge the tables when you're done."

As Matthew worked through the morning, the number of dead Electors kept bothering him. It was not, after all, seven out of 300 million US citizens, it was seven out of 1,076, the number of surveys he had done. And that number represented twice the number of Electors: 538 Democrat plus 538 Republican.

At about 1:30 in the afternoon, Matthew felt he needed a break to do some work on the dead Electors. He thought about going to his office, but worried he might have to field questions from students, so he walked over to the Government Documents section of the library, to work in peace.

He opened his laptop and called up his data on the Electors before logging onto the Census Bureau's Vital Statistics. Once there, he looked up Mortality Rates. The crude death rate in the US was 9 per thousand.

"Damn," he thought, crestfallen. "So here I am thinking something strange is happening and it turns out my seven people dead out of a thousand isn't significant; isn't even above the expected, the average."

Matthew shook his head at himself. "Damn. I'm always doing stuff like this. I have two fewer deaths than would be expected. Big fucking deal. And Winter is probably the worst time of year ..." A thought occurred to him: 9 deaths per thousand was for the whole year. He didn't get the lists until mid-October.

His thoughts rushed: "This is December 5th," he said to himself. "I wouldn't have received the Electors' names at all if they'd been dead earlier. All of these people died between mid-October and the end of November--six weeks." He paused, his thoughts running far ahead of what he knew. He told himself to slow down.

"Okay," he said, beginning again, if nine per thousand are expected to die within a year..."

He scribbled a few calculations in his notebook and looked back at his computer screen for a demographic search of the full and partial respondents. Though he could guess the sex of the dead Electors based on their first names, their race could not be determined by first or last names, though he noted that none of them had Chinese, Southeast Asian or Japanese names. He sighed as he looked at it: even in death Asians were underrepresented.

The seven dead, based on his educated guess coding, divided by sex almost exactly as the living ones had: four were male, three female. Though it was an intellectual leap that someone like Calder might call into question, Matthew decided to assume that the seven dead could be regarded as a faithful random sampling, as merely a miniature demographic snapshot of all the other Electors.

On his laptop screen, not all the columns could be seen at once. Beginning on the left, the first column contained a unique number for each Elector who had responded. The columns that followed were Sex, Race, Age range, Income, Level of Education, the responses to the questions, State in which they voted, and Party. Each column contained only numbers.

As he looked between his screen and the Vital Statistics data, trying to find some means of comparing his data, he became frustrated that he could not see everything. He tried

—

16

the 'hide' feature, which concealed a whole row or column from view without changing or deleting it, but he found that it was worse to have something hidden than merely out of view. There was no census data on whether one's party affiliation had anything to do with one's life expectancy, so he allowed the column containing party affiliation to remain out of view.

The census site had a list of mortality rates arranged by level of education. Matthew sorted his respondents and found that the overwhelming majority had at least attained a two-year degree. When he looked back through the book, the death rate for those with some college degree was four per thousand annually. For his two-month period, that meant 0.67 deaths expected.

He searched by the age group 45 to 55, into which 74 per cent of the Electors fell. The annual mortality rate was still four deaths expected per thousand. The next page gave deaths by accidents. Matthew remembered that his work-study assistant had said four of the Electors had died in accidents. The age group 40 to 45 yielded only 0.033 expected deaths by accident.

Matthew paused. In his mind he heard Professor Calder's voice saying, "There has to be some other connection." Matthew nodded as though Calder were there in the room with him: "You'll earn your money, and your reputation as a scholar, by finding that connection no one else thinks to look for."

Matthew rolled his shoulders to relieve some of the tension he felt and applied himself again to the task--only this time, he attempted to disprove the idea that there was any significance to the deaths.

An hour and a half later, he sat back, staring blankly at his computer screen. For his two-month period, no matter how he ran the numbers for a given group, less than one death was expected. Matthew had seven deaths – unexpected - and certainly unexplained.

CHAPTER THREE

Imogen Trager had just reached the doorway on her way out of the office when the telephone rang. She growled under her breath as she turned, wrestling with the hastily composed stack of files and papers she would need for the meeting. She walked back to her desk. The Assistant Director, Doug Pollack, had sounded harried and scattered when he had called her to the meeting, and she assumed this was he again; that he had just remembered something else he wanted her to bring. But as she flipped a long strand of red hair from her face and leaned over her desk, she saw that the call was from an outside line. She would be late if she took the time to answer, so she let it ring and turned on her elegant, sensible Nine West heels.

As she entered the large hallway of the Bureau's west wing, she tugged at the bottom of her blue suit jacket with her free hand to straighten it over her skirt. The heels clicked with purpose on the heavy stone floor as she marched toward the Assistant Director's office.

"Genny, I need you," Pollack had said when he called. Genny knew all about need. She knew that when the Executive Assistant Director needed something, when he used that specific word, it was because he saw his chances of promotion withering for one reason or another and wanted to delegate something. He had asked her to bring everything she had on the "Illinois Project," his managerial euphemism for the FBI's investigation into ballot tampering in Illinois.

Imogen knew about her own need as well, her need to escape Washington, to escape her quiet, tastefully appointed apartment, the one she had been so sure would be her refuge from the chaos and intrigue of work, but which in the absence of chaos or even compelling work, was no refuge at all, but merely quiet, pedestrian, underused. As she moved along the hallway she saw the possibility of her need for some intriguing work coinciding perfectly with Pollack's need to clear up the Illinois mess as quickly as possible.

As she turned the last corner, she saw Tom Kurtz dart out of his door and into Pollack's office. "Of course," she thought. "They'd send Tom to manage everyone, create reports." Her pace slowed, tentative. She paused six feet short of Pollack's door, rolled her shoulders slightly to loosen them, resettled her glasses, tried to dispense with the disdain she knew was souring her face by the time she stepped through the open office door.

Tom's needs, too, were known to Imogen: his need for constant reassurance, his obsession with power and its application. But she knew also that he was valuable and valued, and on his way up. Imogen had lumped his failings under the rubric "not working out," when she had broken off their brief affair. She had held to stubbornly vague words when they had spoken intimately that last time. When he asked why she was ending the affair, she had given evasive answers, as though to explain her disappointment and boredom might have led to her saying something out of proportion to what she really felt, when what she really felt was that she wasn't feeling enough.

"Thanks for coming, Gen," said Pollack, standing to shake her hand across the desk. Tom stood and shook her hand. "We've got a shit storm in Illinois," said Pollack. "I'm sure you've seen these." He laid a section of *The Washington Post* onto his desk, so that Tom and Imogen could see the headline: "Justice Department Stalled on Ballot Tampering". Then *The New York Times*, which read: "Silence on Tampering Claims".

"I just saw an NBC-*Times* overnight poll that says almost thirty per cent of the public thinks there might be a cover-up," said Pollack. "That's up from eight per cent last week."

"So, has something changed?" asked Imogen. "I read the *Times* piece. I didn't see anything new or particularly damning."

"But there is a perception," said Kurtz.

"And that's the problem," said Pollack. "Genny, I sent your preliminary findings along to the US Attorney's office, and I cc'd the Public Integrity office. Public Integrity said that with no compelling evidence we should wait until the state was done with their investigation, so as not to have a chilling effect—their words—on the election. They didn't want the investigation itself to become a factor in the outcome. We've left it in the hands of the Illinois AG's office up to this point, but now we look bad."

"I suppose the Illinois AG's office regards it as a state matter," sighed Kurtz. "And we've left it to them to burnish their incompetence to a high gloss. Which they have faithfully done."

"Exactly. Last week, I saw no problem letting Jezek from Public Integrity poke around quietly."

"You sent Jezek?" asked Imogen. Her voice betrayed more incredulity than she had meant to reveal.

Kurtz widened his eyes at her and smiled at her faux pas.

"I didn't send him. I agreed that it might be all right to let him go. Christopher conceded a month ago," said Pollack with a helpless shrug. "You said there was nothing conclusive, so yeah, I said OK."

"So, is there something now?" asked Imogen.

"No. As you said, there's nothing new. I mean, yeah, someone from Christopher's office, we think, is agitating the issue. The US Attorney in the Northern District has been getting calls. That's not surprising. And that's how it got into the papers." Pollack tapped the newspapers on his desk. "But because it's in the papers, the Director wants us to look into it."

Douglas Pollack was always taut and wiry, and at the prospect of any impediment to the progress to his career, he became more high-pitched, as though someone were retuning him, making him vibrate with extra energy.

"So, Tom, I'm sending you to Springfield. Gen, I need you to work directly on the statistical data, see what you can make of it. I need you to work closely with Tom, keep him apprised of what you need and why. Tom, the Illinois people aren't going to like this new tack. I leave it to your discretion how you apply pressure to the locals to get what you need. But get it. Your first two days, you're on your own. Thereafter, I want daily reports."

Tom nodded. "With the papers sniffing after us," he asked, "should we minimize our profile or emphasize it?"

"I leave that to you," said Pollack.

"What I mean," continued Kurtz, "is that we could attempt some media damage control, or we could throw them something to chew on."

"It's up to you, but make sure you're on the right side of Public Integrity."

"I mean, if we could show that the locals have been subverting the process...?"

"However it gets done, Tom, but be careful."

As Kurtz stroked his moustache and goatee, Imogen could see him puffing up with the power he was being entrusted with. He smoothed his moustache and pulled gently at the tip of his beard.

She felt she knew what Tom was thinking. Though they had been together only a short time, Tom had talked about it so much: "This is how it works," he would say. "They throw someone like me out into the wilderness, without guides or instructions so that if I fuck up, they can say it was my fault and then make a big show of soul searching, taking blame only for not having supervised me more closely, for having sent someone so green out to do man's work.

22

"So now, all that they've admitted to is an error in judgment, even though by telling me they have absolute faith in me and my discretion they have in essence told me to throw away the rule book and get done whatever needs doing. But I'm smart. I'm good at this. And after I've survived long enough and got results, sooner or later, I get to be the guy who gets to disavow any knowledge of my underling's actions."

It had been on a similar damage-control team that Imogen and Tom had met and been drawn to each other. Tom's confidence, his spin on what he did and its importance to the security of the nation had been intoxicating at first, coming as it did after the first bloom of excitement over her own job had withered. He knew more dirt and intrigue than anyone she had ever met.

She had come to realize that he used the foibles, indiscretions and crimes of others to disguise the emptiness in himself, but at first it had been fun. Directly after the assignment, however, and short of a new challenge, Tom had deflated. He became fearful, tentative. He boasted pathetically and with his insider information even began to sound contemptuous of the ordinary people whose interests he was sworn to uphold.

Imogen wondered about the faint smile now on Tom's face as Pollack talked about how closely the two of them would have to work. Had he seen an opportunity to rekindle their passion?

"Do you want a statement to the press that a new team is going in?" asked Tom. "Can I assume you'll ask to recall Jezek?"

Pollack hesitated, trying to see his next actions from multiple angles.

"As I see it, the department needs to show that it is addressing the problem," Tom continued. "Second, it needs to deflect criticism of the investigation up to now."

"Exactly," said Pollack.

"I understand," said Kurtz.

The men were in vigorous agreement as to how Kurtz should proceed, though nothing had really been said. Jezek would be recalled. Kurtz would bring along some of his hand-picked people, and they would begin their efforts, first letting it be known in the press that Justice was re-doubling its efforts, that the FBI was on the case. There might even be a subtle hint that the previous team had not been up to the job. Kurtz would "apply pressure" as needed, if assistance was not readily forthcoming from the local jurisdictions.

Imogen felt badly about the bubble she was about to burst, but the boys were making things far too complicated. She regarded complexity as a flabby luxury—as something left undone. Her way of tackling problems came from an aesthetic sense of order.

"Look," she began, "from what I understand, to get started the main issue is determining whether the release of the ballots was engineered in some way. Is that correct?"

"Yes," said Pollack.

"All right, then," she said. "The problem is less that we don't have enough data. The problem is that no one has asked the proper questions."

Both men nodded, though they looked puzzled.

"What do you need, Gen?" asked Pollack.

"I still don't have everything I asked for almost a month ago—and maybe that's something Tom can help with; but in order to find tampering, or to give it all a clean bill of health, I will need all of the data from all of the precincts in Illinois. We don't have to involve Public Integrity yet.

"What I need to get this started is to know the precinct results and when they reported them. I need it broken down by the actual time they reported. I need a count of registered voters for each precinct, broken down by party. If there's fraud, I should be able to narrow the scope of inquiry. When

I have narrowed the field, I'll begin to test the reported results from those precincts against the same data from other elections--even for other political offices. If there's fraud, I will be able to point directly toward those who engineered it."

"How?" asked Kurtz, despite himself.

"Using the last two or three elections," Imogen began, "we will create a standard profile or pattern for each precinct—a history, a norm."

Pollack and Kurtz nodded.

"First, as part of that history, we establish whether a given precinct is majority Republican or Democratic. Then, we look at how and when they report, along with the historical percentages for Democratic and Republican candidates. Applying that norm to the current election, we can see whether there's a large deviation, and if there is, we scrutinize those precincts. And I can compare them with other precincts and the times they reported their results."

She paused a moment. Both men seemed to be following her, so she continued. "Okay. It's the Democrats who are accused; so, we look for precincts with historic Democratic majorities and we look particularly at those that are not reporting as expected. Let's say that prior to the late returns, the votes for the Democratic candidate were running at about 55 per cent, and that percentage is consistent with other races."

Both men nodded.

"But then in the late reporting precincts—say, the last ten per cent of the votes counted—the Democratic vote rises to 60 per cent and the climb looks directly linked in time to some late returns from another precinct, where there's a Republican majority. That would be a flag."

"How?" asked Pollack

"Because it would show there was reason to believe that the late returns were padded in some way to defeat the increasing number of opposite votes."

Both men bore the same distasteful expression on their faces. Statistics to prove a fraud? It seemed unmanly, like putting Al Capone behind bars for income tax evasion.

"So our investigating doesn't matter?" Pollack said finally. He didn't care so much about being outmoded as about being able to explain his course of action to the Director and making it sound good.

"You don't call that investigating?" asked Imogen.

"It seems kind of impersonal," Pollack rejoined. "I know you're good at this, Gen, but stats can't tell us everything. When the research, the investigating, is done... then ... then, we will need your special skills."

"It's true statistics can't tell you everything, but they can do this," she said pleasantly. "And I would say the raw data—your investigation, if you will—is telling us how to proceed."

Imogen regarded their silence as a rebuff, though both were merely trying to understand where they fit into the scenario she had just outlined.

"Think of baseball," she said. "At the beginning of the season, what do batting averages mean?"

"Not much. They haven't had enough at-bats."

"Right. Too little data upon which to make a claim or prediction. But by mid-August or so, you can give, say, the batting average for Nelson Cruz or Mike Trout and have it mean something. Or whether, say, a home-run hitter like Mark MacGuire will send it out of the park."

"There are a hundred sixty-two games, Gen. By mid-August they've played around a hundred, and if he's a starting player he's averaged three or four at-bats a game."

"So now not only can you calculate his batting average, you can calculate it against right-handed pitchers or left-handed pitchers; you can calculate it with runners on base, or with runners in scoring position: you can calculate his batting average against right-handers in domed stadiums with men in scoring position on Tuesdays if you like."

Imogen paused.

"My point is that in late innings, in a close game, the manager knows the average, knows the probability of success or failure ... and he acts accordingly."

"But they still have to play the game. The statistics are finally meaningless."

"Are they meaningless, Doug? We amassed the data from their playing the game. Does it demean the talent of either Cruz or Trout to reduce their hitting to numbers?"

"No," said Pollack, "but one of the thrills of the game is watching them beat the odds."

"So the odds do mean something, then. You agree that you get a good picture of a player's ability by looking at his batting average, or fielding percentage."

"Yeah, okay," said Pollack. Kurtz had disengaged from the conversation and was staring off into space, stroking his beard.

"And that, nevertheless, there are still anomalies." asked Imogen. "Slumps and streaks."

"Ye-ess.

"And when such anomalies occur, we attempt to look for the reason. Why is the pattern different ... right?"

"Sure," said Pollack.

"And in that way, history, past work, is relevant."

Pollack nodded.

"Doug, I want to look at the Illinois results from all elections for all offices, past and present; and if I see any anomalies, I'm going to ask why. The patterns, as in baseball, have been established by the game ... in this case this election and past elections are the game. When a precinct doesn't act as it has in the past, perhaps, like Mark MacGuire, they've been juiced ... padding their results."

There was silence. Pollack nodded slowly.

"Once I have that, I can tell Tom directly where to look, which precincts to scrutinize. Then we tell the the USAO and Public Integrity exactly what we need and what we're doing."

Pollack scratched his head. "Tom," he said finally, "Let's hold off on anything in the press. Let Gen do her work, and then, armed with good information about where to start digging, I'll send you to Springfield. Gen, give him a list of what you need. Make sure everything goes through Tom. He's the lead."

"Fine," said Kurtz.

"Okay," said Pollack, rubbing his hands together, suddenly feeling better about this whole business, "I don't know why I didn't think of you two in the first place. It's such a perfect match. Gen, your task, superseding all other duties will be to find sufficient evidence (or its lack) to convene a Grand Jury and/or instigate a full-field investigation. I need daily progress reports from you both. Okay?"

"Yes," said Imogen.

"Uh huh," muttered Kurtz, wondering what the hell he would have to report, since apparently the real work would be done by Imogen.

"How did you come up with all that?" asked Pollack. Kurtz had risen to go, but suddenly felt he should sit down again. Pollack waved him on. "That's all, Tom," he said. "Thank you."

"I'm interested myself," said Kurtz.

"It's what I was hired for, Doug. It's what I do. But the Illinois AG or their State Police must have at least one or two people equally qualified. A better question is, why didn't someone else think of it first?"

Imogen returned to her office and quickly began looking at who in her staff should take what work of hers now that she had been put on the Illinois investigation. She sent an email to Kurtz detailing what she would need to start coding the election data.

"How did you come up with all that?" Pollack had asked. For the first few years of graduate school, Imogen herself had felt dissatisfied with the impersonality of statistical research. Statistics weren't glamorous, and outsiders who didn't understand their capacity to reveal truths often scorned them as reductive of human dignity. Pollack's distaste stemmed from his having to rely on a woman's quiet probing rather than Kurtz's cowboy bravado. Pollack was not such a fool as to refuse help where he found it, but he could still silently mourn the passing of his romantic, gumshoe ways. Statistical evidence was not sexy, even Imogen would have admitted, but for her it had grace, was quietly beautiful.

At the thought of "beauty" her mind flashed to Professor Duncan Calder, her graduate advisor. "When you have created a theory, it must stand the scrutiny of three tests," he had said: "And those are Truth, Beauty and Justice; that is, is it true, does it stand up to challenges? Is it simple, elegant ... is it beautiful? Finally, is it just? Will it harm others needlessly? Most scientists only concern themselves with the first two."

She had been a little in love with him. Here, in a particularly male-dominated field, with its talk of "hard" and "soft" science, of "penetrating logic" and "seminal works" she might easily have failed to find her niche, might have gravitated to something with more initial encouragement, but which left her feeling less than satisfied. Calder had given her the encouragement she needed, had listened patiently to her scholarly problems and crises; had reassured her she had what it took to succeed. He had swayed her. He had, she felt, given a part of himself with his attention, his seemly enthusiasm for what he did.

Calder was a hyper-competent researcher, a professor of

Political Science specializing in elections. He was neither arrogant nor self-consciously humble about his abilities. He was simply working at something he was better at than most people in his field. Imogen had hoped that same sense of assurance and entitlement she so liked in him would grow in her; and today with Kurtz and Pollack she felt it had. She knew better than they did how to begin to conduct this investigation. She was not arrogant. She was not putting them down. She was not making claims for her ability that were unwarranted. She knew exactly what she would do, exactly how she would go about it, and what it would take to do. Moreover, though she would never let on to anyone else, it would be fun.

Again, she heard Calder's words resounding in her head. They had been working late one night, struggling with a problem. She had looked up from her protocol coding and stared at him as he studied the data scrolling down the screen. Though his brow was furrowed by thought and concern, his mouth completely betrayed his mood. He was smiling.

"You look like you're having fun," she had said.

Duncan had looked at her suddenly, his reverie broken. "I'm going to tell you something very important right now," he said. He had looked about the room to see if anyone else was there. "If you love doing something, never, *never*, let anyone know you think it's fun. Otherwise they won't pay you to do it. People in this world are paid to work, not have fun. If work and fun were the same thing, we wouldn't have different words for the concepts. Now promise you will never let on."

Imogen had laughed and raised her hand in mock pledge.

And now, yes, while she cared about whether there had been fraud in Illinois, her zeal for the work had more to do with finding an answer to a problem than with potentially uncovering a conspiracy. And in its odd way, it would be fun.

CHAPTER FOUR

Professor Calder sat at his desk, staring at his computer. "I suppose I could try to get Yamashita by email," he thought. It was after lunchtime, and Calder had already stopped by Matthew's office in the bowels of the Political Science building but hadn't found him. He had called Matthew twice, and had even left a message in Matthew's box at the main office. He drummed his fingers next to the keyboard.

Calder logged on and sent: "Matthew: See me--Calder."

There was an urgent ping from the pocket of his sport jacket.

Calder pulled out his phone. It was a text message from Matthew.

"Duncan," it said, "I need to show you something."

Calder gripped the phone and typed, "everything ok with the surveys?"

"yes," Matthew texted. "done. but I've come across what looks like a conspiracy."

Calder threw back his head and let out a deep sigh. Another conspiracy? he thought. "excellent news about the surveys," he typed, not inclined to go into Matthew's conspiracy theories. Calder remembered all too well Matthew's claim that he could demonstrate that there was a coordinated Republican-led effort to dumb-down the nation by attacking education at every level.

"I'll model it for you and send it along later."

"OK," Calder typed, dreading it. "And the surveys, they ready to go after next lecture?"

"yes. no problem."

Both men lay down their phones and sat back in their chairs, Matthew in the library, Calder in his office. The

---

interchange had not gone as either would have liked.

More than twenty years after he wrote them, Calder's first publications on the effect of the Electoral College with respect to leadership, allocation of campaign resources, turnout and strategy remained required reading in the field of American Politics. His insights and models had stood the test of time. Tenure had followed. He did as he liked and followed his research interests. Along with finding an intellectual home at the University of Washington, he found Seattle suited him too. His divorce, five years before, however, had left him beached, with no one to share his breakthroughs and the faculty gossip.

His mentoring and relationship with Matthew Yamashita had been special from the start. Calder liked the quickness of Matthew's mind, his ability to grasp complexity but not be overwhelmed by it. On the day Matthew was accepted into the graduate program at the University of Washington, he had phoned Calder at home, practically crying as he said that his family would not allow him to take the position even though it was fully funded. Calder had offered to fly to the Bay Area to speak with Matthew's parents. "There's a conference in San Francisco I was planning on missing, but it seems perfectly timed now. I'll be there," he had said.

When they met, at the home of Hiro and Claire Yamashita Richmond, California, Matthew's parents were polite but cold, clearly regarding Calder's intercession as interference in family affairs that were already settled. Calder pleaded his and Matthew's case admirably, touching on the stability of an academic career, its modest prestige, its autonomy.

"Think about it," said Calder, screwing up his courage for the next mouthful of natto, a Japanese delicacy no one in the family enjoyed or had eaten in years. "As a lawyer, you're on the clock. It might be a well-paid clock; but you have to account for your billable hours. For a JD you go to school for three years past your undergraduate work minimum, slog through your first few years as an associate—everything that anyone who is a professional has to endure—and yet, at the end of it, no matter how high you climb, you must submit to the clock. A person pulls himself or herself up into the professions precisely to avoid this kind of nonsense; and not merely for money—though money counts, too—but for freedom, autonomy and respect. For happiness."

All eyes were on Calder as he slid his chopsticks under the natto and delicately lifted the fermented soy beans to his mouth. A thin, viscous strand, like dewy spider silk drew upward from beneath his chopsticks as he raised the natto to his lips. And as it neared, the heady smell of the fermented beans filling his sinuses, the slickness and chalky malt taste still coating the inside of his mouth from the previous bite, proved too much. Calder quickly plunged his chopsticks into his rice to cover the scent and swallowed the mixture.

"Why do we work?" he asked as he swallowed hard, trying to appear as though he were approaching the problem from another angle.

"To make money," answered the elder Yamashita. "So as not to be a parasite, a boil on the backside of the family that brought you into this world."

"Good," said Duncan, somewhat taken aback. "Okay. Good... and when you have a skill that is in demand?"

"You get the highest price you can get for it," Matthew's father said.

"So money is a way of keeping track of what is important?"

"The only way," said Yamashita Sr.

"All right," said Calder. "The university has paid for part of my airfare to come down here. They are offering Matthew much more, I think, than a law school might."

"I can pay for Law School, professor."

"Yes. Yes, of course you can. But a state-funded,

---

research-one university is willing to spend money on your son for you. How many Law Schools are clamoring to do that?"

He was enjoying the sparring more than the natto, but he could not help wishing he had been so much in control when he had confronted his own father years ago.

After dinner, Matthew's father invited Duncan onto the back deck to enjoy the summer evening. Duncan commented on the view. Matthew's father nodded gruffly. "You like Scotch?" he asked, not waiting for an answer before pouring him a glass. Duncan noticed the bottle of single malt whiskey. "Oban? I love it."

Matthew's father walked to the far rail of the deck and leaned against it, one foot on the lowest rail. Duncan followed.

Matthew's father took a long drink. Without turning to Duncan he said: "I want you to know that every argument you made tonight my son has already made."

Duncan stared down, scenting defeat.

"I was not persuaded by those arguments from my son, and I was not persuaded by them coming from you."

Duncan attempted to interject, but Matthew's father held up his hand: "What does persuade me is that you felt he was important enough to come down here."

"He is important."

"Is he that good?" asked Hiro, his tone a mixture of pride and dismay.

"We'll see. There are no guarantees. But he has more going in than most have."

Matthew's father nodded and took another long drink.

Duncan leaned against the rail, his right foot resting on the bottom rail, a perfect mirror of Matthew's father. He too took a long drink. "Are you going to tell Matthew while I'm here, or should I wait for him to call me with the good news when I get home?"

"I haven't decided that part yet." Yamashita smiled and took another drink.

The two men had remained on the deck until much of the whiskey was gone, talking about everything and nothing, about Yamashita's own business, his hopes for Matthew. Finally, with the sun at its lowest point, Matthew and his mother, unable to bear the suspense, had come out onto the deck.

Hiro Yamashita turned heavily toward his wife. "Claire," he had said, "get two more glasses. I believe a consensus has been reached."

Matthew, standing almost at attention, looked from his father's face to Duncan and then back to his father, his face registering the rapidly evolving emotions within him, from shock to gratitude, to giddy joy.

So Matthew had become a graduate student in the Political Science department, and under Calder's tutelage he had done exceptionally well. He had published three articles, had begun giving papers at a number of conferences and had become generally regarded as one of the department's up-and-coming stars.

Matthew's success—and the questions he asked—had energized Calder. Now, though, at the beginning of his third year of graduate school, Matthew's relationship with Calder had changed. Each had found limitations in the other. While the mutual esteem remained, layers of bland accusation and irritation had built up on top of the respect, like sediment in a still lake, blurring the lines that defined them. What was left was the surface rather than the depth of their relationship, silting it under with what each regarded as limitations in the other.

Matthew felt that Calder was unable to care or become involved in matters that pertained to people; that he was interested in them only as numerical abstractions. For his part, Calder sometimes regarded Matthew as frivolous, involving himself and expending his spirit in areas that had nothing to do with his studies; and his conspiracy theories— about the assault on education, the gun lobby, housing bubbles were becoming a liability.

In their disagreements, Calder felt tremors in Matthew's recriminations which seemed to be running to the same themes as those which had brought about his divorce. The accusations were painfully similar. Calder was incapable of action, Matthew would say. Unable to fully connect. He was incapable of relating to what most people regarded as "the real world."

Early in his career he had joked about it, believing it was a strength: "The real world is a sham," he had been fond of saying in seminar. "The constant calls by the public, the legislature and the media for relevance to the so-called real world are just code, meaning we should dumb down our interpretations, make them responsive only to business and politicians. If that's the real world, I don't much care for it. That's why we're here: to see behind the facade that pretends to be the substance. I'll leave the real world to others." But Calder could no longer support his interpretation of the silence which followed this pronouncement as agreement. He knew it was polite dissent.

Now, Calder sat in his office and cringed inwardly to think how many times he had claimed that the real world was a fiction, picking at the scab of his hubris. Meanwhile, Matthew sat in the library establishing the numbers that would prove the significance of the deaths.

Two hours later, when he walked over to Calder's office, the professor was gone. He cursed under his breath and went back to his own office. From his laptop he copied and downloaded all of the vital information, including the sites listing gross death rates.

Why the hell wasn't Calder there? He tried the home number. No answer. The information Matthew possessed burned in him. His work to show definitively that there was a conspiracy had simultaneously energized and unnerved him. He had to tell someone else. But who should he tell? The police? The F.B.I.? He had to share this. The deaths had happened across the nation. It certainly wasn't a matter for local police.

Someone at the F.B.I or the Justice Department or the National Security Council must be looking into a rash of deaths like this. Matthew suddenly remembered Calder's words to him when he began the survey: that he was the only person tracking all the Electors.

Were the authorities in on it? he wondered. How wide did this go? How could he reveal what he knew and be safe? Who could he tell?

He considered sending his findings to everyone in his email address book; or to prominent Political Science departments in the country. "But what if I'm wrong?" he thought. He saw himself a few years down the road, or rather he saw his CV being put straight in the "Definitely Not" pile by some smirking search committee member. He had to have Calder look at these findings. Where was the old fool?

Matthew ripped open the center drawer of his metal desk and began pushing aside pieces of paper, bar coasters with notes on them, pens, paper clips. At the back, a little crushed, he found it: a business card for Jerry Ingram, a former grad student who had left during Matthew's first year and was now at *The Washington Post*.

Matthew called Ingram's number. "Hi, Jerry, this is Matthew Yamashita at U-Dub. You may remember I helped with some research on a story you wrote about HUD a few years ago. Anyway, I've got something I think will interest you, and it's big. I've been doing a survey of Electors for my dissertation on party identification, and I've come across a number of deaths. Too many of the Electors have died—it can't be a coincidence—and no one seems to be looking into

---

37

it. I can't see a pattern yet, but too many have died for this to be a coincidence. I'm pretty sure some of them have been killed. Call me any time day or night. It's 9.30 your time."

Afraid of losing the data, he burned it onto a thumb-drive, which he put in an envelope and put in his file cabinet drawer. He emailed the data set to Calder, too. Then he set off for the College Inn Pub.

Less than half an hour later in a bar in Washington, D.C., junior political reporters were hanging around, joking about their editors and swapping stories, when Jerry Ingram sensed a lull and excused himself to check his messages. Rather than rejoin his colleagues, he sat at a separate table and began scrolling through his contacts list looking for someone he could call to corroborate any of what Matthew's message had just told him. When he found his "source", he called immediately.

"Yes, it's me. Sorry about the time. I just got a call about someone killing Electors. Sounds like it could be important. It's a grad student at the University of Washington. He was surveying all the Electors when he came across it. I wondered if you've heard anything about it or... Sure. Of course. Where do you want to meet? I can be there in ten minutes."

Ingram hung up, and then immediately began a text to Matthew: "Matt, thanks for the lead. I'm meeting with a source at Justice later tonight. Will be in touch."

Safe in the rathskeller that was the College Inn Pub, Matthew gave himself over to beer. He wandered into the back, where the news was showing.

"Finally, tonight," said the anchor, "we return to Illinois. While James Christopher has given his concession speech, there remain doubts about the outcome of the vote tampering investigation by the Illinois Secretary of State. Why is it so important? These 20 Electoral votes could upset the whole election, robbing Diane Redmond of the presidency and giving it to the challenger, James Christopher. You will recall there was only a four vote difference between them."

"They're wasting their time," Matthew said to no one in particular. This was bigger than some corruption in Illinois, he thought. His phone pinged, and he read Ingram's text. Matthew smiled, sighed with relief and ordered another beer.

Next day, the political editor at *The Washington Post* decided he should write the eulogy himself. He hadn't known Ingram for long, but he had been a reliable reporter and had broken several stories. Ingram had died when the car he was driving hit a tree in the small hours. The blood-alcohol content in his scorched body was .12

Matthew rolled out of bed with his alarm at 9:30 the next morning. Sitting on the edge of his bed, he called Ingram's cell. Not getting an answer, he immediately dialed the office phone at the *Post.*

"Washington Post," said a young woman's voice.

"Hello, I was looking for Jerry Ingram. I thought this was his number."

"It is, sir. Or, it was."

"Was?"

"May I ask who's calling?"

"My name's Matthew Yamishita, we went to school together. I talked with him yesterday."

"I'm sorry to be the one to tell you, sir, but Jerry is dead. He died in a car accident late last night."

"I see. An accident?" Matthew could hardly believe what he was told. He had left his message less than 12 hours before, and now the man was dead.

Matthew walked through the rest of the morning bewildered. Had he administered the kiss of death by calling Ingram? he wondered, and would he be condemning anyone else he told? Could it have been merely an accident?

He became frantic as the day progressed, his delirium made worse by not knowing who he should talk to next. He was frightened. He had been right, and this was confirmation. He felt He must be in danger too—but from whom? He called Calder's number twice and stopped by his office three times. He didn't come on to campus on the days he wasn't lecturing, but where was he?

He considered calling his parents, but knew how they would react. They were trustworthy, of course, but they would not be able to cope with responsibility like this. They would try to calm him down while panicking themselves. The last thing he needed was a domestic crisis on top of the trouble he was in already.

In the harsh light of an unexplained and continuing series of deaths, his graduate student colleagues suddenly looked frivolous and ineffective. Faculty other than Calder were not close to him; and while any of them would have understood the scope of what he had uncovered, he could not trust them to act. For that matter, he might not be able to trust Calder to act. But Calder had to know. Presumably he *did* know by now, if he had opened his email. Why was there no reply, and where was the old fool?

That afternoon the Illinois Secretary of State called for help from the United States' Justice Department in its investigation of voter tampering, and the National Affairs editor of *The Washington Post* commissioned a weekend feature about drinking and driving in America.

Matthew knew none of this, and he would never know. As he left campus that night, having sequestered himself for the second half of the day, proud of himself for having gotten back on top of the bubble, having avoided one more crisis, he decided not to stop at the Pub but to ride home and collapse, to sleep.

The weight of his knowledge was a burden; but he

would talk with Calder in the morning. Calder was always in early on the days he lectured. Maybe he would read his email and need desperately to speak with Matthew...

It was a full moon, though in Seattle no one could tell. Had there been less cloud cover, Matthew might have seen a faint glint of chrome or flash of new paint as the car darted out beside him. As his bicycle headed into the heart of the Arboretum, the dark blue car very neatly and rather quietly drove him headlong into the side of the brick footpath bridge over Lake Washington Boulevard. The car continued. Someone came out of the shadows behind the bridge, felt for a pulse, took Matthew's laptop, searched his pockets for keys and walked away.

CHAPTER FIVE

December 10, 2016: Seattle

Calder frowned as he strode into the lecture room, wondering where Yamashita was. Matthew was due to give the lecture for class the next day and go over the initial findings from the group assignment. Calder wanted to see it first.

Professor Calder regarded the formulaic approach to lectures as the best. In his mind, the progression of a lecture was very much like a car trip: begin by backing out of the garage with a little reversing: "Last time," he would invariably begin, "we discussed..." First gear was the introduction of the three main points he would cover in that day's lecture; tying these in some way to the previous lecture gave a sense of smooth second gear. This morning as he was in third gear, approaching cruising speed and the shift up into fourth when a student's hand went up, a stop sign in the middle of nowhere.

"Professor Calder, I just heard on the news that the Justice Department has been called in to assist the Illinois Secretary of State in the investigation of vote tampering. Do you think this will have any effect on the outcome of the election?"

"Probably not," said Calder confidently, anxious to get on with his lecture. "That is to say, it is a mighty big ask. I mean, *if* they can prove the tampering on only one side, the President-elect's, *and* they can prove the tampering altered the overall Illinois result, then Illinois' Electoral College votes go to Christopher, and Christopher wins ... but I'm afraid that's not likely to happen."

"Why?"

Calder sighed inwardly. "If they do a thorough inquiry, it will require scrutiny of all the results, and this being

---

42

Illinois, I can't imagine either major party wants a lot of scrutiny. Chicago and the northern part of the state is reliably Democratic, but the southern part is staunchly Republican."

"Would our surveys be helpful in some way?"

"I don't see how. I'm afraid the surveys will not be very useful for predicting such things. Those surveys are strictly demographic studies. As you know, Mr. Yamashita ... who is not here today ... Matthew and I decided to combine his dissertation work with a class assignment.

"I thought it would be productive because, one: you would learn directly how surveys were conducted; two: you would gain knowledge of their structural constraints—not to mention the benefits to Mr. Yamashita's dissertation; and three: because in the last class, there had been a number of questions regarding the Electors themselves.

"The students in that class last year had been struck by the fact that Electors were more important decision-makers than many of them had previously thought. When I attempted to give some general comments based upon who these people, these Electors, were, I could find no data on who comprises the slate of Electors. The class and I were struck by how very important the Electors are and how little anyone knows about them. Who are these people and how do they get to play such a crucial role in what we think of as a popular election? So I decided that a demographic survey would be useful and interesting, which is what some of you have been doing with Mr. Yamashita."

Another hand went up, and Calder watched his well-laid lecture plan slide farther from view. "But how are Electors decision-makers?" asked the student. "What decision do any of them have to make. It's a rubber stamp. A formality."

"Yes and no," said Calder.

"Don't Electors have to vote the way the state went?"

"No," said Calder.

"No?" asked the student. "But I thought..."

"We have gone over this before..." Calder began, not unkindly.

"Okay," he began. "You know already that the people do not vote directly for the office of President. We cast our votes, and within each state, whichever candidate receives the largest popular vote—a plurality, not necessarily a majority--receives all of the Electoral votes that state carries. The number of votes each state has is equal to its total representation in Congress—its number of state Representatives plus its two Senators.

"Here, in Washington State, we have ten Representatives and, like every other state, two Senators—which gives us twelve Electoral votes." He wasn't sure how much ground he should cover again, but he decided he was right to begin at the beginning.

"But it is not our representatives who cast these votes, but Electors, who meet in the state capitols across the country on the first Monday after the second Wednesday in December, as determined in the Constitution." Calder paused and looked at his syllabus, lying open on the lectern. The dates for each week of the quarter were listed on the left-hand side.

"This year," he said, checking with the list, "that first Monday falls on December 19th—exactly nine days from today. The Electors then formally and officially cast their votes for the President of the United States. There must be an absolute majority of Electoral votes to secure the Presidency—270 or more.

"If there is no absolute majority, which is mathematically possible, it goes to the House, where each state gets one vote. Think about that. If there was no absolute majority and the election went to the House, the congressional representatives of each state would have to agree on either the Republican or the Democratic candidate.

Presumably the small states with only three representatives would have a simpler task agreeing who they support, but can you imagine the chaos in California, with 53 representatives? Or New York state, or Florida? Pennsylvania? Illinois?

Calder looked about the room, waiting for a hand to go up, or to see a quizzical look. Seeing nothing but rows of laptop lids, their apples glowing mute consensus at him as their half-hidden owners tapped away, he went on.

"As it currently works, each political party chooses its 'slate' of Electors in each state. To use Washington as our example again, this means that the Democrats in Washington State choose 12 Electors and the Republicans choose their 12; the Revolutionary Communist Party chooses 12, the Libertarians choose 12, and so does every other party that has advanced a candidate for President.

"Each party member is pledged to vote as he or she has agreed to vote, if their party's candidate receives the plurality of votes in the given state, except in Maine and Nebraska where they use a plurality by district as well as state. So, in this election, in Washington State, Diane Redmond narrowly won a plurality, so the Democratic Electors will go to Olympia on the first Monday after the second Wednesday in December—the 19th—and vote for her in the ultimate round of the election—the one that actually decides who will be President. All of the other Electors in this state stay home."

Pointing to the student who had asked about Electors, he said, "Your question, your quandary, is the result of this current party system which rubberstamps the process of electing the president, when the original intent was that Electors be decision-makers."

The class were looking expectantly still. "In the last class I taught, students became uncomfortable with how little was known about who Electors are. They realized that in principle the Electors have much more power as decision-makers than we imagine." Some heads looked up and nodded.

"Now," he began again, "this is where it gets interesting. Even though this system of 'slates' of Electors is the system we all more or less know, there is no Constitutional provision that says an Elector must vote as he or she has pledged to vote. Nor any Constitutional Amendment. The current method of electing the President is a product of states writing their own rules. We can talk about why they did that another time, if you'd like, because that's also quite interesting.

"But the system most of you thought you knew before you began this class is not the system that is outlined in Article Two, Section One of the Constitution of the United States on electing the President."

"There's no Amendment?" asked a student.

"Only the Twelfth, which merely clarifies some of the rules about the vice-president. It makes no mention whatsoever of the people voting for President, or having any influence over the process. Like Article Two, Section One, it speaks only of the Electors meeting to cast their votes for President in the capitols of their respective states—not even in Washington, DC, because of the logistics of travel in those early days."

Calder felt himself in high gear. He burned with two discreet passions, both of which were pleasurable: the one was to remain focused and answer the student's question with as little digression as possible; the other was to tell them everything he knew, right there and now, to get them to feel the same love and awe he felt for his subject.

The danger was that everything he knew had been built on 47 years of living and absorbing; and in his mind everything was relevant and interconnected. He considered telling the class about the states' reasons for the current system; he considered talking about the former power of the two parties; he thought he might invoke Andrew Jackson's failed attempt to get just such a Constitutional Amendment passed. But the clock showed he was running out of time by allowing his thoughts to stray. For a moment, he glimpsed himself being dragged from the classroom in a strait-jacket, spouting ecstatically about voting fraud in Louisiana and Texas, spewing anecdotes about Lyndon Johnson, Ben Franklin and the Long brothers.

Another student raised his hand. "Yeah. But professor, come on. Even if there's no Constitutional provision..."

"The weight of censure and mistrust will keep the Faithless Elector from ever breaking his pledge?"

"I guess not," said the student. "Right?"

Another hand went up. "Faithless Elector?"

"One who goes against his or her pledge and votes differently than expected," said Calder.

"And there's no law?"

"There is no Constitutional Amendment nor provision. Many states make it a legal requirement to vote as pledged, but no one knows whether those requirements would be ruled Constitutional if they were challenged."

"But something must happen to them."

"In 1976, Gerald Ford, running against Jimmy Carter, won here in Washington State. But Ford received only ten Electoral votes instead of the –then—eleven votes Washington State carried. Mike Padden, a Republican Party Elector, voted instead for Ronald Reagan, who had run during the primaries, but had not won his party's nomination."

"What happened to Padden?"

"He later ran successfully for the state legislature as a Republican," said Calder. "I think he recently retired."

Suddenly feeling he might be letting an opportunity slip by, he went on: "The term 'Faithless Elector' might be misleading somewhat, because as originally designed they were intended to be decision-makers, faithful only to their individual consciences."

"But it didn't matter to the outcome ... those switched votes?" asked the student.

"No. No," said Calder. "Not at all. Gerald Ford had already lost by much more than a one-vote margin. Padden's was largely a protest vote. It didn't matter to the outcome. A switched vote has never mattered to the outcome."

Matthew was not in his office when Calder tried it after the lecture. He wanted to see Matthew's work, but he wanted also to talk with him about the unusual turn his lecture had taken. He called Matthew's cell, asking for a call back the moment Matthew received the message.

He banged the receiver into its cradle. He stared at the computer, hesitated, and then logged on. The only message from Matthew was from two days earlier, its subject line reading "electoral conspiracy". In exasperation, he deleted it without reading it and spun quickly around in his chair to glare out the window. "Damn his little theories. The university is going to get tired of funding his paranoia."

It was a rare sunny December morning. Flat, gray light scattered everywhere. The light streaming through Professor Calder's window did not warm what it touched; rather it leached color, left no shadows, as though the entire city of Seattle were under interrogation.

Not wanting to start anything new before he got to work with Matthew, he busied himself with answering emails, flagging those he would need to revisit, dropping ongoing issues into various folders, deleting others. He cleared his spam folder, cleared his "trash", and then set to work on the papers on his desk, discarding papers, putting others into piles for further attention, or to be filed.

There was a knock before the department secretary entered, shoulders stooped by the weight of her news.

"I didn't want to call," she began. "It seemed so impersonal. So...." She looked around the room, looked at the bookshelves as though scanning for a title she wanted. She looked at anything but at Duncan. "Matthew is dead," she said, her eyes fleetingly meeting his.

"What?

"The police just called."

"How? When?"

"Last night, they say. On his bike. Hit and run." She paused. "They say it happened right by the footbridge in the Arboretum late last night. I'm sorry, Duncan." Her heart went out to him. Seeing the grief he tried so hard to keep to himself made her like him for the first time in their long association.

She was crying now, and after a moment Duncan came around from his desk, his legs carrying him automatically. He felt nothing. Even numbness is a sensation; but this feeling was no feeling at all. He wasn't even sure he was in his own body. He moved stiffly to console her. Looking at his arms as they closed around her shoulders, he almost wondered whose arms they were. After a moment they both regained their composure and withdrew from one another.

"His parents know?" asked Duncan, grasping for anything that might belie his feelings. Feeling nothing, though eerie, was preferable to the sudden feeling that overcame him in his chest of crumbling, like dry-rotted sheet rock, the hole growing ever larger as the back of the hammer gouged and ripped.

She nodded. "The police called them first."

"I'll call them, too. I'll make sure that Mr. and Mrs. Yamashita know that if they need anything, they should talk with me. Anything at all," he repeated absently and began walking toward his desk. Calder paused at the corner of his desk and leaned on it. He stared out at the bleak day.

"Thank you for coming personally, Beryle. Hearing it over the phone would've..."

49

Beryle left quickly. It had seemed Duncan was about to cry.

Duncan sat down at his desk, staring flatly at nothing. Though an atheist by nature and training, he alternately thanked whatever it may have been that had spared him children of his own, and then with rancor equal to this gratitude, cursed the fragility of life. "Not Matthew," he whispered aloud, as though he quite easily might have understood the death of someone else.

Though the rotting hole within him continued to grow, he was outwardly much more himself as he finally rose from his desk and walked out into the hall. There was still work to be done. And he would take on Matthew's share.

The idea of having to teach Matthew's sections filled him with dread, but he had to keep on. He owed Matthew so much, and he knew of no way to show it, nor to whom he should repay it unless to the other students.

He went to the department office. "Beryle," he asked, "who do I see about getting into Matthew's office? I figure I should pick up and continue whatever he was doing."

"I'll get the master key," she said.

Duncan walked heavily through the maze of hallways in the basement of Gowen Hall. He stopped at Matthew's door. Tacked and taped across Matthew's door was a mass of cartoons and photocopied ephemera. Duncan scanned them, noticing them properly for the first time.

A couple of Doonesbury cartoons set in classrooms; a single-panel cartoon in which a student wonders aloud "if we stop taking notes, do you shut up?"; a satirical treatise from Teachers for a Democratic Culture which dictated Regulations for Literary Criticism. Regulation VII caught Duncan's eye: "No irony."

He put the master key in the door and opened it. Matthew's office was cleaner than Duncan had expected. Gone were the piles he was used to seeing, the clutter, the papers spreading across the floor. Where were the surveys? he wondered. Matthew's desk was bare except for a phone charger cord duct-taped to the formica topped desk. He must have taken everything home with him to work there.

The following afternoon, December 11, Hiro Yamashita came to Duncan's office. Both men were pale and haggard. Hiro had barely slept in two days. Duncan had stayed up late to prepare to teach Matthew's section, and had slept poorly when finally he did get to bed.

Hiro had come for his son's body, and he needed Duncan's help to pick up the debris of Matthew's life. He was formal, though distracted. His sentences often went nowhere. Duncan recognized in him an air similar to the look that had greeted him in the mirror that morning when he went to shave: an air that was not resignation to what came next, but of profound indifference to whatever came next.

"I have some bluebooks and papers," Matthew's father began.

Duncan took them. "Thank you."

"I figured ..."

"It was very kind. You really didn't need to. I'd have come to help if I'd known. You have enough to deal with."

"Claire wants me to get ... whatever I can to bring home. Stuff he did. Papers he wrote ... you know."

Duncan nodded. "I'll take you down to his office now."

Matthew's father nodded.

"Is that all you found at his apartment?" Duncan asked as they walked down the stairs toward Matthew's office.

"All that had any relevance to school," he said. "I sat there in the middle of it all, putting things Claire wanted in one pile, stuff you'd probably need in another and throwing the rest into another pile to be thrown out." He paused, halting on the stairs.

"I'm sorry you didn't call me. I'd have—

51

Hiro shook his head slowly. After a moment, they continued down the stairs and along the hallway.

Duncan opened the door.

Hiro looked around quickly. "Where's his computer?" he asked immediately. "Claire wanted it. He loved that thing, wrote all kinds of stuff on it. She wanted those things."

"Yeah, he took it everywhere."

"It wasn't with him when he got hit," said Hiro, "and neither were his keys."

"His keys?"

"No. I had to get his landlady to let me in."

"Did you find any surveys?"

"Everything I found that had anything to do with school—even if I didn't know if it was for school—I brought to you. We could go back there," said Hiro, clearly not wanting to. "What would it have looked like?"

"You couldn't have missed it. It would have been a huge pile of questionnaires. Probably about two reams of paper. If we don't have his computer, we could at least reconstruct his work from them."

"I didn't see anything like that. Was it really important?"

Duncan nodded. They went back to Matthew's apartment.

Matthew's father hung back as Duncan opened drawers and file cabinets, preferring to remain in the kitchen.

The questionnaires were not there. "Thank you for letting me come," said Duncan.

"I have to come back tomorrow, anyway," said Matthew's father. "To get all this packed up. I told his landlady to keep whatever furniture and stuff she can use ... his damage deposit. The idea of ..."

Duncan nodded. "I'd like to keep in touch. If there's anything I can do for you, please call." The two men shook hands and walked to their cars, each still stunned by the perversity of young death and struggling to adjust to a

—

different future. Internally, each accused himself vaguely for things not done, things that might have tipped the world just enough to be otherwise.

Where could the surveys be? Where was his laptop? Duncan wondered as he got into his car to drive back to campus. It was possible to imagine that someone had found Matthew after the accident and stolen his computer. His keys could have been knocked out of his pocket on impact—but why hadn't the police found them? And where were the surveys?

Calder turned right, onto Lake Washington Boulevard and drove through the Arboretum. Calder slowed as he approached the footpath bridge where Matthew had died. He parked in a gravel parking lot near the bridge.

There were still remnants of yellow police tape knotted along a few branches at the site where Matthew had been hit. In the fading light, the spot looked peaceful, benevolent. As he walked along the road, Calder tried to conjure the moment when Matthew died. He looked at the road, the guardrail leading up to the bridge. His footsteps drew him along Matthew's final moments. He stepped into the road and stood by the guardrail, peering under a tree, presumably the spot where Matthew's body had come to rest.

The guardrail would have made it impossible for Matthew to escape the car. Had he noticed the car at practically any other spot, he might have jumped his bike over the curb to get out of the way. But here, there was no escape. Duncan felt sick.

A car honked at Calder as it made a wide arc around him. Calder was still standing in the road. He stepped over the guardrail, under a low branch. He crouched in the space under the tree where Matthew's body had laid and reached down. The ground under the tree was thick with wet leaves and mud. He grasped a handful of leaves and slowly crushed them in his hand. They were slimy and gritty. Calder fell to

---

his hands and knees and began patting and shifting the leaves, looking for anything of Matthew's. Water from an overhanging branch dripped onto the back of his neck as he pushed deeper under the tree and into some bushes. Calder turned to sit on the ground and gathered his knees to his chest. It was cold, quiet. The still December air was redolent with the musky scent of decay.

CHAPTER SIX

December 12, 2016

The next day and a half were particularly frenzied and difficult for Duncan as he made changes to the course. He found himself missing Matthew horribly. More than just the young man himself, Duncan had relied on Matthew's ability to take on whatever Duncan needed him to take on. He had grown accustomed to the quickness of Matthew's mind; and while the other graduate students were by no means dull, he had not the history with them he had with Matthew, the ability to communicate in shorthand language, the experience that allows one to leap far forward from a mere sentence.

As he had hoped it would, throwing himself into work had helped push down the pain of Matthew's death. Perhaps things might get better, he mused as he stared out his window at the darkened campus. Calder liked the campus at night. Quiet, there was still an air of purpose about it, reverberations of the ideas and enthusiasms of young minds.

Things might return to normal, he allowed, though with that thought came the dread of what had been normal, the inanity and irrelevance of his life before Matthew came to the university. He had relied upon Matthew so much—maybe too much, he concluded. Matthew had been worthy, and would have become a great scholar, but Duncan felt he should take more responsibility for himself.

He was no longer staring out the window, but at a wall. His musings had gone on for almost half an hour. He checked his watch. It was past midnight. Duncan turned back to his desk and stared again at the papers he would now need typed and copied. He yawned as he stretched. He shook off his fatigue and collected the papers.

Duncan put on his jacket and scarf, turned off the light and walked down the narrow corridor toward the main hall. Just as he joined the main hallway, he stopped and looked back, feeling there was someone else around. But he saw no one.

Duncan looked again. He had heard nothing, but he could not shake the feeling there was someone nearby. He continued on toward the main office, unlocking the heavy metal door and pulling it open with the key in the lock. It slammed shut behind him with a heavy metal bang that made him jump.

"Okay," he thought to himself with a smile, "maybe I don't like being here all alone after all." His footsteps echoed lightly. He walked to the side of the office, paper-clipped the papers he wanted scanned and copied and placed them in the "work" box and then headed toward the men's bathroom. As he washed his hands and threw his scarf over his shoulder, he realized he had no gloves. He patted the pockets of his blazer and his mind suddenly flashed upon them. In his mind, he saw them perfectly, sitting innocently next to the computer in his office.

Duncan took care not to let the door slam this time as he left the main office. The idea of it slamming and echoing throughout the building filled him with dread. Just as the door clicked locked and he turned to head back to his office, he heard a door slam. He quickened his pace because it sounded as though it were near his own office. He saw no one in the main hallway. As he entered the corridor to his own office, he saw the back of someone going out the doorway at the opposite end.

It was not one of his colleagues. Two women and two men occupied the four offices along that hall. It clearly was neither of his male colleagues nor the significant other of either of his female colleagues.

The man walked quickly to the door.

"Can I help you?" Calder called out.

The man's pace slowed. For a moment, the man seemed about to look back but quickly checked himself and continued his quick, though unhurried walk to the double doors at the far end of the hallway. He vanished from sight the moment he was beyond the doors.

Duncan's hands shook as he opened his office door. Once inside, he turned on the light. Nothing was gone. He reached for his gloves. But they were not there next to the computer. As he tapped around his desk absently, he inadvertently touched the top of his computer monitor. It was warm. He felt his heart race wildly, beating sickeningly, unevenly. A moment later he found the gloves on the floor at the side of the desk opposite from where he felt sure he had left them. He stood next to his desk, the only sound his own fast breathing. Duncan dialed the campus police.

The campus police arrived presently. Duncan felt he could detect in their expressions their frustration with him for not having had a better look at the suspect. The best he could give them was: "Six feet tall, short black hair, collar length; gray tweed jacket, pale blue collared shirt, khaki slacks."

"We'll look into it, of course, professor," one of the policemen said, "but that describes a lot of people on this campus."

The other officer looked Calder up and down for a moment. "That describes you, in fact," he said. "Perfectly."

Duncan looked down at what he was wearing. He figured that if he were robbing campus offices, he'd try to look like someone who belonged too. His mind suddenly returned to what he had said in lecture a few days earlier about vote tampering; how anyone involved in wrongdoing would seek to minimize their exposure, would seek to minimize their profile. Anything odd or out-of-the-ordinary made people curious.

"Well," said the policeman, "you're lucky nothing's gone.

57

I'd be careful, though. I mean, no sign of forced entry ...
We'll alert the main office that a master key has been stolen
again. At the moment, I'm afraid, there isn't much else we
can do."

"I knew my description probably wouldn't be of much
help," Professor Calder said. "I wanted more to alert you that
at the very least this building is being cased."

The police left, and Duncan sat down at his brown
swivel chair. He looked again around his office. Nothing was
missing, but he could not help feeling that something had
changed. Calder pulled on his gloves, wrapped his scarf
about him again and went out into the night.

No moon shone through the low layer of clouds. The
wind, though it rustled the leaves on the trees he passed, did
not penetrate his jacket, nor could he feel it brush against his
face. He stopped at the parking lot between Thomson Hall
and the Student Union Building. The brown light issuing
from the street lamps glittered across the wet asphalt.
Nothing moved. There was no person but him, no sound.

It disturbed and upset him to realize the thief looked so
nondescript; that he had, as the policeman pointed out,
looked like Duncan. "How would you know danger when it
came?" he wondered to himself, "when the thieves look like
us?"

He paused again. His car was parked on the bottom level
of the three-tiered parking lot under Padelford Hall. Under
the best of circumstances the stairs down to the parking lot
were daunting. Tonight, they were frightening. Duncan
slowly descended the stairs next to the stopped up escalator.
He found himself wishing he could cast his ears forward, like
a cat, so that he might hear danger coming. His footsteps
echoed lightly. There was no other sound.

As Duncan reached his car, his emotions were that odd
mixture of relief and self-accusation--relief at having
accomplished the task, and recrimination at having been so

afraid of something so easily accomplished. He started his car and drove downtown. The garage door under the apartment complex near Pike Place Market opened as he pressed the button on the handheld remote clipped to the passenger-side sun visor.

He paused just inside to allow the door to close completely before continuing to his reserved parking spot. As the metal door touched the ground, sending a muffled clang resonating throughout the garage, Duncan exhaled deeply, feeling safe for the first time in hours. It was 2:30 in the morning.

Inside his condominium, Duncan threw his keys on the table just inside the door, hung his jacket on a hanger in the closet and walked through to the living room. Duncan went into the kitchen and rinsed the heavy-bottomed glass standing next to the sink. He shook out the water and then opened the cupboard behind him.

He took out a bottle of Oban, single malt and poured his customary two fingers into the glass. He put the top back onto the bottle and was about to replace it in the cupboard when he pulled it down from the shelf again and poured another finger or so. Duncan stared at the glass for some time, blank. He poured a trickle more, but left the bottle out.

It had been years since Duncan had been awake this late and not been drunk. He had no idea what to do with himself. He walked out to his balcony overlooking Western Avenue and gazed to his left at the Public Market, sleeping now. The wind he had not felt while walking to his car was now up, swirling small bits of garbage at street level, tousling his hair and nipping at his cheeks on the fifth floor. A car passed from time to time, but no one walked. He took another drink of whiskey to fight off the chill in the air. As he came in off the balcony and closed the door, the warmth inside suddenly made him very tired. He sat on his sofa and stared at the television remote control, wondering if he had the energy to turn it on.

Calder's apartment was long and narrow with high ceilings, what are called "shotgun apartments" or "railroad flats" when they lack a commanding view or are inhabited by those of less means than valued professors. It was spare and clean, monochromatic. Everything in the apartment was white, or black or chrome, clean and angular, functional but not invitingly comfortable.

After his divorce, Duncan had decided his new life must be different from his previous life, not merely a repeat of his bachelor days. He had banished all clutter from his life. Without the warmth of books on the wall opposite the couch, the apartment might have been said to have no personality at all.

For the first time in some years, Duncan felt the lack of vitality in his surroundings. "I hate my apartment," he said to himself as he rose from the couch to pour another two fingers of whiskey into his glass. Even the word sounded uninviting. "Apartment," he thought. It reminded him of something. "Apartness," he said aloud. "or apportionment ... increment". Duncan took a long sip from his glass: "My incremental apartness has been apportioned..." He held his glass in the palm of his hand, examining it, as though if he stared at it long enough he might clarify his ennui.

He placed the glass next to the sink, precisely where he had found it, leaving the last swallow untouched, and went to bed. As Duncan trudged to the bathroom, three fruit flies abandoned their sugar search, having found the mother lode in his glass. They promptly paid with their lives for their gluttony.

Duncan stripped to his boxers, carefully placing his clothes in the hamper to be washed by the cleaning woman who came once a week to dust, vacuum and take his clothes to the cleaner. He went to the bathroom and began brushing his teeth.

His loneliness seemed augmented by his gleaming bathroom. There were no toothpaste stains on the tile surrounding the sink, no film covered the basin. The hand towels were hung evenly, gently overlapping across their gleaming rods. There were no mystifying, clarifying lotions, night creams or eye gellees crowding at the corner, no suggestion that makeup had ever been applied. The garbage bin next to the toilet was empty. Even the drain top was clean. Duncan stared at it as though that was the last straw.

He did not miss his wife, but he missed the clutter that another person causes. He missed not being able to talk when he came home. He missed not being able to talk about his day, to hear about hers. He missed the clarification and perspective that comes from having talked with someone else.

As Duncan studied himself in the mirror, white foam bubbling from his mouth, he felt acutely his lack of understanding of the night's events. He was missing something, he was sure. Having someone to speak with might have helped him draw it out.

Duncan finished brushing his teeth and began studying himself in the mirror. Why didn't he have anyone? he wondered. He wasn't hard to look at, he graciously admitted to himself. He was in good shape for a man his age. He had no paunch at the belly, only the slight thickening at the waist which seemed representative of his age, unavoidable in that sense. His chest did not sag. There was definition in the muscles of his arms. His legs were strong and solid. They had always been so. He was intelligent ....

Duncan left off this cataloguing of virtues as pointless. His ex-wife was right, he thought. He was self-centered, seeing only how someone else might benefit him. He was pining for someone to talk with not because he wished to be taken out of himself, not because he wished to submerge thoughts of his own trials and tribulations, but because he wanted to find something out for himself. He wanted someone there only because he needed someone else to hear him talk.

Duncan turned back the covers of his bed and scooted his body between the sheets. The bed was cold and hard, the sheets rough. The whiskey had worked. Now, he was not only tired, but sleepy, too. By the time the alcohol wore off, he would be sound asleep. Duncan nuzzled his pillow, pressing his cheek deep into its firm austerity, hoping to dream of springy flesh, of full-figured, intelligent women who never cleaned up, whose scent filled his sinuses, heady, like the dust from which we were created and to which we must ultimately return.

Just as sleep was almost upon him, Calder's eyes started open. Why had his computer monitor been warm? he wondered. He hadn't used his computer all day. And why had his gloves, which had been right next to the keyboard, been on the floor? Duncan sat up out of bed, bringing his feet to the floor. He wished there were someone next to him who would come awake and ask, "What is it?"

"My computer," he said aloud. "That guy was looking through my files. He could have corrupted my data, erased things, planted a virus." Duncan was now pacing beside the bed, "Jesus Christ," he thought. "Years of work, statistical evidence. Why would someone do that? What have they done? And, whoever that was, he was a pro. That's the only explanation for why he didn't turn around. He heard me when I called to him. He's well-disciplined, certainly. He knew that if he turned around, I'd be able to identify him. Who would do this? Jesus, I'll never sleep now."

The thief had clearly been in the office, whoever he was, not to steal anything but to look for something. What could he have wanted? Calder's computer had been warm. He had looked through his computer. What was he looking for?

Duncan had his trousers on now and was getting ready to

leave. He was angry. What if it had been some hacker? He would never know when his whole hard drive might seize up. Who hates me so much that they would want to corrupt my data? he thought.

He parked in the lot between Thomson Hall and the Student Union Building. A campus police squad car cruised by slowly on the main road but did not stop. "Of course not," thought Duncan, "I look the part, just as whoever broke into my office looked the part." He walked quickly to his office.

Once inside the front door, he walked quietly toward the little hallway that led to his. Duncan unlocked his door quietly and pushed it open quickly, throwing on the light. But his office was just as he had left it. Duncan took stock of his office. The monitor on his computer was no longer warm, though it had been, so perhaps whoever it was had found out all he needed to find out with that one visit.

But what could he have wanted? What secret did Calder know that was of any use to someone else? He was a scholar! When he knew something, he told everyone who would listen.

Duncan decided to start where his intruder had started, with the computer. Fear, however, was teaching him to be paranoid. He made as though to leave, picking up some file from his desk, and walked to the door where he turned out the light. In the darkness, he skulked back to the window and peered out. There was no one on the path between Gowen Hall and the library, no one anywhere.

He turned the light back on. Though this did not purge his anxiety and anger, it was comforting. Gone were the shadows and lurking darkness which seemed to expand and contract as though the whole room were breathing with the same quick, unmeasured breath of its principle occupant.

He turned on his computer and waited as it went through the normal start-up routine. When it was finished, he looked to see which application was highlighted. He reasoned that whatever was highlighted would be the last thing used, and if it didn't correspond with what he remembered using last, he might gain a clue. Excel was highlighted. He felt certain it was not the last thing he had used, though he could not recall what the last thing had been.

Email perhaps? He clicked on the campus email. As the email screen came up for him to log on, Duncan looked in the upper right-hand corner. Duncan was confused. The "last login" date and time were for December 12 at 4:08 p.m. He had been in his office at the time. He knew it.

Someone had somehow captured his password and had read through his email remotely. But they couldn't check his hard drive remotely, and so had been forced to break into his office to look at what he had. And they had gone to Excel to look for whatever it was they thought he had. Why?

Back in Windows, Calder opened Excel and clicked on 'open recent'. None of the files, though, was anything he could recall having worked on recently, but they were each of them studies in one way or another of political party loyalty.

As Calder scrolled through coded protocols looking for changes or obvious errors such as a neophyte hacker-Sociologist might make, he remembered that Matthew, like himself often wrote out statistical data in Excel before mapping it over the standard statistical program S.P.S.S. One or two of the files the intruder had looked at had been sent to him from Matthew via email. In fact, Matthew had probably initially coded the Elector protocols in Excel. As he continued, opening files he hadn't looked at in as much as six months, he mused on the possibility of someone thinking his research was seditious; but that was absurd.

A chill ran through him, as though some icy finger had just lightly traced its way up the back of his neck. Matthew had said he had data about some conspiracy. Maybe he had stumbled on to something. Calder pushed his chair away

---

from his desk. "No, no, no," he said aloud, attempting to clear his mind. "No," he said again. There couldn't be anything to Matthew's claims. Calder stood up and began pacing behind his desk. "Goddamnit," he hissed, as though attempting to shut up the rush of thoughts afflicting him. He sat down again. "Facts. I need facts. This is stupid. It's insane!"

The facts, however, were not much help: Matthew said that he had uncovered evidence of a conspiracy among his data on Electors; Matthew was now dead, and all of the evidence with which Calder might have disproved Matthew's argument had vanished--the uncoded protocols, the coded reference file, Matthew's laptop. Someone had logged on to Calder's own email and read it; and someone had broken into his office. All of this had happened within a few days. Was it wrong to suppose there was a connection?

He stopped himself. This was no way for an eminent academic to be thinking. The only reason he did not understand was because he had not asked the proper question. No information upon which to pose a sound question, however, was available without some version of Matthew's protocols. Matthew's research was the key to proving or disproving what was suddenly so tempting to believe.

Matthew had indeed probably entered the data from the surveys on the Electors in Excel, which he could do on his laptop computer before mapping it over into SPSS. Duncan felt a shudder. "In fact," he thought, "Matthew might have sent the file with the protocols by email, telling me how and where to extract the file. He's done it before." Duncan's heart fell sickeningly. If Matthew had sent the file, it was attached to the email message Duncan had deleted without reading.

CHAPTER SEVEN

December 13, 2016

Calder waited impatiently for the university's day to begin. Since the time he had been a graduate student, he had never been on campus before 9 a.m. He had even complained about having to teach the Intro to American Politics class that quarter because it met at 9:30.

As he sat in his office that morning, watching the clock on his desk turn from 5:30 to 6 and then to 7 a.m., however, this knowledge did little to ameliorate his feeling of injustice at the frivolity and lack of work ethic among his colleagues. His zeal to find out what Matthew had sent made him anxious to find a way to retrieve deleted email.

He dimly remembered a graduate student once asking him to sign a petition about the uses and potential abuses of email archives—something to do with privacy. The discussion that had ensued had been illuminating, if frustrating. Duncan had not liked the graduate student's tone of patient exasperation, like one who tries to explain something simple to an otherwise precocious child who at the moment is not trying hard enough.

"Okay," Duncan had asked, glancing at the petition, "but how can someone read your email?"

"They don't have to be at your computer," said the graduate student.

"I know that, but wouldn't they have to know the user name and password?"

"Yes."

"Then how do they get in?"

The student had looked stunned.

"All right," Duncan began. "I'm clearly missing something."

The student nodded. "The problem, professor, is that email is in a central archive. At the central archive, they already know your user name and password because that's where you created it."

"Well," said Calder, taking the petition, "that does change things."

"Thank you professor. This is important. They could even read things you've deleted."

At the time, Calder did not want to ask how, feeling that he had exposed enough of his ignorance for one day. He only shook is head, as though he couldn't believe the depths to which some people might sink.

That had been perhaps three years ago. Calder found himself hoping the petition had gone nowhere and that it was indeed possible to access deleted messages. He had in mind a particular colleague, David Stinson, who seemed so cyber-spaced, so taken with the tricks his machine could do, that Calder sometimes wondered why the man ever bothered coming to work. He hoped Stinson could help, and that he wasn't still sore about Duncan's crack at a faculty dinner party about sometimes wishing that Stinson were only virtually real. But Stinson wouldn't be in for hours yet.

Calder had hoped that preparing for lecture that day would help him pass the time, but as he had taught the course before and had his lectures largely mapped out, this took only about five minutes. The sleepiness he had experienced at about 2.30 was gone, replaced by a slow adrenaline burn, which kept him awake, if not alert. Though he didn't quite feel it, Duncan knew he was tired.

The world presented to him was jagged and rough, though fuzzy edged, as if every object within his field of vision had suddenly become porous and swollen with water—though oddly this did nothing to blunt the sharp edges and corners he constantly bumped or inadvertently kicked on his regular forays from his desk to the hallway to check for activity. The flat, hazy light of morning hurt his eyes when he left his office to get some coffee at 7.30.

There were a few students about now, as he walked from Gowen Hall to the cafeteria of the Student Union Building. He felt he should know them by the way they seemed to stare at him, but they were all undergraduates, so he was fairly confident he did not know any of them well. Nevertheless, they did seem to stare.

Duncan went to the bathroom on the main floor before going down to the basement for coffee. At the sink he ran cold water over his hands and rubbed it across his face. He looked in the mirror. The hazel-green eyes had dulled. Normally, they dominated his face as the first and last thing people remembered of him. Under normal circumstances, his face had a healthy pallor, a pale glow framed by dark black hair, from which his eyes shone.

Now, he looked as though he had been on a bender. His face was no longer pale but ruddy. Under his eyes, the soft skin was purplish-red. His beard, now a day old, added to the perception that Calder had let himself go. He threw some more water on his face, but still there was no change. "Gonna be a great day," he sighed as he looked at the mirror.

In the basement cafeteria, Calder bought the largest cup of coffee they offered. It was thin and bitter and scalded his tongue, which helped with the taste. He trudged back the way he had come, knowing it was still too early for any of his colleagues. Back at his desk, he momentarily considered napping for an hour or so, but decided against it as too risky before having to lecture. At 9 a.m. he took a tour of the offices in Gowen, and, still finding none of his colleagues in, went back to collect his papers and went early to lecture.

Lecture seemed to have gone well, he thought as he left the classroom, but he was damned if he could remember a single thing he had said. He would definitely need some sleep. It was 10.30 a.m. and he rushed back to his office. He threw his folder and papers on top of the file cabinet next to his desk. He picked up the phone before he was seated and dialed Stinson.

Professor Stinson picked up on the second ring.

"David?" said Calder, "It's Duncan. Listen are you going to be there awhile? I have a question for you."

"Sure, Dunc. I'll be here for at least the next forty-five minutes."

"Perfect," said Calder and hung up. The frenzy to get to the bottom of all this was on him again, stripping his fatigue from him like a wet shirt that is ripped off and wadded up. His rush for the door wasn't slowed by his old distaste for his colleague, nor even by being called "Dunc".

Stinson's use of the space in his standard-issue university office still rather bewildered and offended Calder. He sat not at the standard heavy, black-metal, Formica-topped desk, but at a light, white-topped drafting table, directly adjacent to which was a bright metal rack on casters, housing the proliferation of computer equipment Stinson thought he needed. Even Matthew had found it daunting and a little silly, though he coveted the multiple screens Stinson used. Matthew had once noted that Stinson's setup looked more like the stage equipment for a rock 'n' roll show than necessary tools for a professor's intricate calculations. "If you look close enough," Duncan remembered Matthew saying, "I'd bet money he has a dry ice machine."

"Dunc," said Stinson as Calder knocked and entered. "What can I do for you?"

"Well, I need a little help. I thought of you as the best person to ask."

"I'm flattered," said Stinson, who, having looked up

69

briefly from his screens, now quickly checked his phone and looked back to the screens.

"You see," Duncan began, not sure if he should wait for Stinson to give him his full attention or whether it might ever be forthcoming, "I'm having a bit of difficulty with email."

"Oh! Don't even start. It's medieval, this system. I hate it. How do they expect us to get any work done? Ben was just commiserating with me about that very thing. I told him you said 'hello', by the way."

"Ben Seidel?"

Stinson nodded.

"How is he?" asked Calder, despite himself.

"Fine," said Stinson, "though Linda doesn't sound so happy. He says she feels cut off in New Zealand, though I don't know why since their bandwidth and baud rate are so much better than ours. I guess they've been fighting."

Unsure how bandwidth—let alone bawd rate—could dispel feelings of isolation, Duncan feared he might be about to learn more about the couple's marital relations than he wished to know. He held up his hand. "Of course moving so far from home was a risk . . . but I'm sure they'll work it out. His research is going well?" he asked, trying to turn the conversation into a new direction.

"I guess so, but he does whine about her."

"Of course, that's between them . . . and you, I guess."

Duncan began to have misgivings. Stinson wore his indiscretion like a mantle of cosmopolitanism. Duncan told himself he would have to be very careful what he said. A gossip with the world at his fingertips was no longer merely an annoyance. And Calder did not want the world to know that he was foolishly pursuing information on so fantastic a scheme as a conspiracy about Electors.

"So what's your problem, Dunc? Do you need to update your equipment at last?"

"Actually, I need help figuring out how to retrieve something."

"It ought to be pretty straightforward," said Stinson.

"That's what I'm hoping; but of course it's often true that a thing is not straightforward until you know how to do it."

"I copy that, Dunc." Stinson nodded gravely.

"So," began Calder, "what I need to know is how to retrieve an email that I deleted by mistake."

"Oh. That is the worst. I tell people. I tell everyone. Everyone who will listen. You've gotta back up your data. Dunc, you have no idea the horror stories I've heard. Dissertation info lost, women's telephone numbers . . . the list is endless."

"Endless?" said Duncan. The strain of controlling himself, of feeling that he had to put up with being called "Dunc" indefinitely was almost more than Calder could endure.

"Endless," assented Stinson.

"I'd love to hear about it. I'm sure there are some interesting stories"

Stinson nodded vigorously.

"But right now, I'm under some time constraints. Is there a means by which to retrieve deleted data?"

"Isn't it just in your deleted email box?" asked Stinson.

"I clear everything at the end of each day—trash, spam, everything. It's actually been a good practice up to now."

"Hmm," said Stinson. "Well, you can still retrieve it, but you gotta go over to the Computing and Communications building in person. Can you believe that? In person?"

"Okay. Why?"

"Well, there was some worry about privacy, and how easily someone could access email correspondence . . . I guess there was even a petition sent around. I doubt you knew anything about it. But there was some hoo-ha about privacy or something, which is why you have to go in person, show I.D."

"I actually signed the petition, David. That's how I knew there might be a possibility of retrieving the data."

"Oh, well. You know all about it. Why did you come to me?

"I didn't know who to go to. And how can they find the document?"

"It isn't really erased."

"You mean it goes through that whole routine of asking if I'm sure I want to delete, like it's my last chance, and then it isn't deleted...even though I deleted it from my deleted file?"

"Right. It works exactly the same way on your P.C. The filename . . . like the title, Dunc . . . is erased, which is how the computer finds the file. But the data that make up the file aren't really erased unless you de-frag or it gets overwritten. Unless your hard drive is really full, it might not be written over for some time. That's how you find it."

"So what do I do, David?"

"Go to Computing and Communications. It's in the basement. You have to fill out some forms, swear the email was sent to you; show I.D. It's all terribly slow."

"That's it?"

"Hardly. The first part is the bureaucracy, the thing the internet will tear down, make obsolete."

"So what else do I need to provide them?"

"If you have a range of dates of when the email was sent, that would be good. Some key words, phrases."

"Okay. Thank you, David." Duncan began to walk to the door.

"Pretty important, is it?" asked Stinson.

"Maybe. We'll see." He was at the door now.

"Let me know how it goes," said Stinson as Duncan pushed open the office door.

—

"Yes," said Duncan. "Yes, of course. And thank you." He left quickly, heading straight for the Communications Building. Along the way, he cast his mind back to when he had seen the email message.

"Okay," he said to himself as he walked, "Today is December 13th. Matthew's message was sent either the 8th or the 9th. Key words? What could those be? 'Electors'? Definitely. 'Survey' would be good. 'Deaths'? That might be in there, but why tip my hand?"

The work-study student at the front desk of Computing and Communications made no attempt to hide the fact that Professor Calder had interrupted something more interesting. As soon as he had handed Calder the form to fill out for retrieving the deleted email, he returned to his keyboard. His fingers gave their rapid commands in short, staccato bursts between pauses, his facial expressions offering a running narrative of how well the machine responded to his bidding. First, there would be the quick clicking of keys, then a pause, his face hopeful; a moment later the hope would be dashed, his face would fall, he would consider a moment, then be clicking again.

Calder finished filling in the form, took out his driver's license and faculty card, and pushed them across the desk. The student, absorbed by whatever was not working on his screen, did not immediately notice Duncan was done. Calder cleared his throat.

"Oh. Okay," said the student, rolling away from his computer. "Done, huh?"

"Yes. What else do you need? Do key words help with the search, an approximate date it was sent?"

"All of the above," said the student, grabbing a Post-It pad. At Calder's direction, he printed very neatly, "electors" and "surveys, December 8th or 9th." He stuck the note to the second copy of the order form..

"When will I know it's been found . . . if it's been

found?" asked Calder.

"We'll email you."

"You wouldn't call me?"

The student behind the desk looked quizzical, as though such an idea had never occurred to him. "We usually just put it back in your email box, and then email you that it's there. I suppose we could call you."

"Please do," said Duncan. "I need this information." He wrote down his cell number.

"Yeah, okay."

Duncan's car was parked directly outside the door to the basement of CMU. He had forgotten it completely. As he walked up to it, he saw four parking tickets under the driver's side wiper. He shook his head at his own stupidity.

Now that he had accomplished the task that had roused him from bed, he felt suddenly very tired. He piled into the car, throwing the tickets onto the front passenger seat and drove home, where he collapsed across his bed. He awoke briefly at about noon, took off his clothes and got under the covers.

Whatever pleasant dreams he might have hoped to have were not forthcoming. Instead, he saw himself standing over Matthew's broken body in the Arboretum, the wet leaves slimy, sticking to his face and hands, the musky scent of decay filling his senses.

The phone was ringing.

"Yes. Yes. Hello?" said Duncan into the telephone. "Yes?"

"We were able to retrieve your message. It's back in your inbox. "

"Thank you," said Duncan. "Thank you very much." He looked at the clock—5.30. "That was fast. Thank you."

"Yeah, well. The key words search you gave helped the most. It was from the seventh, by the way."

"Great. So it's just there now?" Duncan paused at the

stupidity of his last question. He was not yet fully awake.

"Right," said the voice at the other end, before the click.

Duncan had eaten nothing all day. There was nothing easy to make in the refrigerator, so he opted to drive back to campus and get something in the cafeteria. He would be there in his office all night, again.

Back in his office, two large coffees huddled together on top of the file cabinet next to his sandwich. He logged on to email. The message was there. Duncan opened it.

"Duncan," it began, "the data on the Electors from the surveys is attached. I think you will agree that it is significant. Here, informally, are the gross death rates, and the death rates by demographic group obtained from U.S. Vital Statistics." Duncan printed the whole message, which included Matthew's models.

He opened the charts he had just downloaded. Calder found a thumb-drive and saved the data to the drive, which he put in his breast pocket. From time to time as he worked through the charts he would touch his breast pocket, as though the drive were a good luck charm.

Duncan had forestalled judgment until he had Matthew's data. He had played a psychological game, telling himself that there was an alternative explanation for what had happened, and this research was necessary only to disprove Matthew's fanciful theory about a conspiracy involving Electors. However, as he worked, his eyes moving from the printed text on his desk to the data on the screen and back, the misgivings he had kept at bay crept through him. His chest felt tight, his spine numb as he pulled out a scratch pad.

His heart knocked hollowly against his ribs as he began writing the data out for himself. "Seven Electors dead," he wrote. He checked that his names and the states in which they lived corresponded with Matthew's data on the printed email. "Seven dead," he repeated aloud. "Seven out of 1,076." He paused.

"Gross death rate per thousand," he said as he wrote, "nine." "Damn," he said as he continued writing "...just on crude death rate there six or seven more deaths than be seen as normal, or expected."

Calder went to the bottom of the worksheet, where the demographic tabulations had been totaled. "Median income...." he wrote.

As he worked through each of Matthew's calculations, he came up with exactly the same numbers. There was no obvious explanation for the deaths, no dubious calculations, no missing steps in the logic to get to the conclusion. Unless he was missing something, Matthew was right. Someone was killing Electors. And that someone had probably killed Matthew, too.

True to his nature and training, however, Duncan put away the sheet of paper he had used to follow Matthew's work, and began again. This time, his hands trembled, his stomach felt empty. He looked over at his file cabinet and realized he still had not eaten his sandwich and that by now, the coffees were cold. "Take a break," he thought to himself. "Clear your head."

But he couldn't, because of a rising fear. Now that he knew what Matthew had known before he died, was he too in danger? Here and now? As he stood, eating his sandwich over the top of the file cabinet, he studied his office, its isolation, its narrowness. The only way out was the entrance through which danger might come in. It was now 7.30. There was no one left on in the building. He suddenly felt very cold, trapped.

"How would I get out of here, if I had to?" he wondered. As he chewed his sandwich, studying the surroundings, he wondered about the window. Was it too high?

He opened it and peered down. Gowen Hall was on a hill that sloped away from the front entrance. If his office had been nearer the front of the building, he could have easily

---

leapt out of the window. From here, though, it was an eight or nine foot drop to the juniper bushes directly below. He opened the window wider. It would be easy to climb out, but he would then have to turn around and grab hold of the ledge, let himself dangle to full length, kick his feet away from the side of the building and push off to clear the bushes. He would probably fall on his ass, he thought, but it could be done. And he would be off and running. He pulled the window almost to closing and went back to his sandwich, pleased at least that he had an idea of what to do.

Back to his task. "Okay," he said aloud and picked up his pen. "I've gone over Matthew's calculations. We've tested by gross population, accidental death, sex, age, occupation, median income." Calder stared at the screen and then looked down at the email printout of Matthew's methodology. "You didn't finish up," said Calder, ostensibly to Matthew. "You didn't control for party."

Duncan scrolled through the data beginning with the name uppermost on his list. For the dead Electors, there was only coding for Name, Sex, State and Party. The rest of the columns were coded "9" for "not ascertained."

Calder sorted the dead Electors rows into one column. As Matthew had found, the fields on the spreadsheet took up too much space to see them all on the screen. Calder collapsed all the fields, so that only Name, Sex, State and Party showed. "Oh, fuck," he whispered. He wiped his palms on the front of his shirt and picked up the pen. He put down the pen and stared at the screen.

All of the names of the dead Electors had a 'D' next to them. Calder, sick with dread, sprang from his desk to look out the window. No one was there. "Oh, Matthew," he said.

Calder could barely think. "Why only one party? What the hell is going on?" He looked out the window again, was about to sit down, but decided to go to the hallway to see if anyone was about. It was 8:45 and the hallway was deserted.

77

On his way back to his desk, Calder picked up the booklet which held the new class assignment. It contained a map, color-coded, showing which candidate had won each state. Calder opened the booklet to that map, and placed it alongside the sheet where he had written the state in which each dead Elector had resided.

Calder looked at the first name. The dead man was from Maine. "Maine went with Redmond, Democrat," whispered to himself. He looked at the next name and state. "Massachusetts . . . Democrat. She lived in Iowa," he said of the next name, "and Iowa went Democrat. I know Oregon went Democrat." He made checkmarks next to each name, ending with Washington state, which had also gone to the Democrats.

Calder sat back from his desk. Conservatively, he had five or six deaths more than expected, no matter how he crunched the numbers; they were all members of the same political party, and they had all died in states where there had been a Democratic plurality. No more than one had died in any given state. "Some circumstantial evidence indeed," he said to himself, remembering Thoreau.

Calder felt panic rising within him. He would have to be smart, if he wanted to stay alive. He forced himself to breath deeply. He focused on making a plan. He grabbed a second thumb-drive and copied the data onto it. He placed that disk inside the waistband of his boxer shorts. He walked to the department office, where he removed the first copy of the disk from his breast pocket, switched on the secretary's computer, and printed Matthew's data. He walked to the photocopier and copied each sheet, including the scratch paper and notes he had written.

From the supply room in the back, he took a manila envelope, on which he wrote his address. He put the first disk and the photocopies into this envelope and sealed it. Then he put the originals into another manila envelope, which he closed with only the metal clasp. As he left the department office, the heavy metal door slammed behind him, making him jump, upsetting the calm he had forced onto himself.

He had gotten away so far, he thought, because they had been unable to find out if he had the information. They had not found it in his email, and they had not found it on his hard drive. Two deaths in the same department would cause suspicion, so they—whoever they were—would be reluctant to kill him unless they were sure they had to. Or so he hoped. But who was doing this?

Back in his own office, he brought up the Excel file again and backed it up onto a disk, which he put in an envelope. He then deleted the file from his hard drive. He exited Excel and immediately reopened the application. He clicked on File. There, as the last thing he had opened, even though it was deleted, was Matthew's data. He opened four worksheets at random, exited Excel and then opened it again. He clicked File. Matthew's data was gone.

Calder looked around the office for anything else that might tip his hand. Whoever was doing all this was thorough. He would have to be just as thorough if he meant to stay alive. He opened the center drawer and took out two stamps and stuck them on to the envelope addressed to himself. While he wasn't sure how safe it would be to mail it to himself, the idea of saving a copy away from himself seemed the best thing to do. He wished he knew and trusted someone else enough to send it to, but he could think of no one he would wish to burden with something that might get them killed.

He felt the underside of his center desk drawer. Too obvious. His desk was deep, however, and the drawer didn't reach the back. Calder found a roll of masking tape, crouched down and taped the second envelope to the underside of the desk directly behind the drawer, well out of sight.

Calder sat down and took stock. He had the information

saved in three places, but the only guarantee that it would save him was if he told someone else.

Had Matthew told someone else? Who could Calder trust? He thought of the FBI, the Secret Service. Had Matthew tried to alert one of them? How had the conspirators found out about Matthew?

Calder cradled his face in his hands. This was too big for local police, and while the likelihood of FBI or Secret Service involvement in the plot was small, trusting either of them could be fatal if they were.

The image of Matthew's body, broken and forlorn floated up again into Calder's mind. Matthew was too good to see wasted like that, his promise too strong. Calder had not been so disappointed since Imogen Trager decided to leave academia to work for the FBI.

That was it! "Genny," he said aloud. Not only could she be trusted, she would know what to do. Perhaps the Justice Department already had something on this? Perhaps they were in the dark because they didn't understand what the statistics meant and hadn't brought Imogen in yet. Maybe he could collaborate with them and shine some light. Together they might begin to generate answers rather than more questions.

Calder smiled wryly at his earlier fear, at his constant window checking, his pauses to listen to what might be happening in the hallway. Genny would help. His ignorance had bought him time. They didn't think he knew anything. Now that he did know they were up to something, they had perhaps moved on, no longer viewed him as a threat. That mistake would buy him the time to speak with Genny, show her the information and to figure out who was doing this.

He threw on his jacket, stuffed the copy he would mail to himself under his arm, patted his middle to make sure the drive had not shifted, and rushed out the door. He headed east toward the Padelford parking lot.

Just off the path between Gowen Hall and Suzzallo Library, down some steps that led to what had been an entrance to the first addition to the library, a man sat on a stone bench. He looked up as Calder hurried to his car. The man stood up, but did not move until Calder had turned the corner at Thomson Hall. The man touched his ear and whispered something. By the time Calder had reached the mailbox outside the Student Union Building, a light was burning again in his office.

CHAPTER EIGHT

December 14, 2016

At four o'clock that afternoon, after numerous meetings with staff who would now take on her work-load so she could focus on the Illinois results, Imogen began putting together the things she would need. On a corner of her desk she began making a tidy pile of folders next to her computer. She looked at the pile, taking stock of what was there, trying to decide if she needed anything else.

She proceeded through her tasks as she would through an intricate mathematical calculation, in discreet increments, from one term to the next, making sure each part was sound before moving to the next. If done properly, as with an equation, there would be a Gestalt solution of glittering, unassailable integrity, a beauty she admired more than anything but had difficulty communicating to others, with the exception of Professor Calder.

She did not look the part of "the math geek," as she was called behind her back by those who envied her swift rise through the department. At thirty-five, she was attractive and energetic. Her delicate hands and uncomplicated face belied the agility of her mind. When she was new to the department, many a man had found himself lingering over Imogen's features during long meetings, her face with its clear green eyes, thin, straight nose, softly framed by rich, deep red hair, streaked here and there with strawberry blonde—only to be jolted from his reverie by a direct question or sharp look.

Imogen had finished most of her work in preparation for the next morning. There were one or two things left to do, but the message light on her telephone was staring at her, and she turned to the calls she had let ring through to voice mail. She took out a drafting pencil, tore the top sheet off a notepad and began listening to the messages.

Surprisingly, the first was from Duncan Calder, calling from a pay-phone outside his apartment building. "Hi Genny, it's Duncan ... Duncan Calder. It's about nine forty-five in the morning your time. I've stumbled across something, and I need your help. I don't want to give details just at the moment. Please call me as soon as you get this message. It's urgent. I'm leaving home now, and I'll be at my office until three and back at home after about four waiting for your call. My office number, is--"

Before Calder could recite his office number, Imogen was writing it down. She wrote down his home number from memory too, before checking them against Duncan's words. She circled both with satisfaction, having remembered them perfectly, and saved the message.

Though she listened to the other messages, jotting down what she needed, she was distracted. There had been something anxious, even desperate in Duncan's voice as he said "I need your help."

She had heard his voice only in her memory during the five years since finishing her Ph.D. She used it not so much to remind herself of Calder, but as a tool: for reassuring authority; for his gentle aphorisms regarding the importance of her work; as a source of praise from someone who knew how hard the task had been. Useful or irritating, our mentors' voices persist. Rather than immediately calling him, she replayed the message.

The last time she had seen Professor Calder, he was in the final stages of his divorce. Her heart had gone out to him. To see him so lost, so betrayed, so subdued was heartbreaking. He did not talk about his personal life, and he was embarrassed whenever others talked about theirs; but his distraction and flat, empty stares spoke for him, dampened the brave face he contrived to put on the proceedings.

Imogen had wanted to comfort him then, to soothe his spirit, but the constraints of their respective roles made any kind of intimacy impossible. Now, he needed her.

Calder sat at his desk staring at the telephone. He had rushed to work at eight-thirty, arriving at his office at nine, certain that he had missed Imogen's call. He had hastily made an airline reservation for later that day. For the better part of the morning he had variously stared at or pretended to ignore the phone. He could not recall having been so anxious in some time. Apart from the fear he felt for his own life, there was a strange mounting tension that had nothing to do with being in danger. He realized he just wanted to hear Imogen's voice.

Although they had spoken on the telephone once or twice since she moved to Washington D.C., the last time he had seen her had been at dinner the night before she left. At dinner, in the restaurant on the ground floor of his building, she had been less triumphant about the successful defense of her dissertation a couple of days before than concerned with how he was feeling and what help he might need after his impending divorce.

Sitting now in his office waiting for the phone to ring, he cringed at the memory of how transparent he had been that night. His feelings were his own business, he told himself. It had been rotten of him to burden someone who had every right to be gloriously happy; who was on the brink of enjoying the rewards of hard work.

"I'm fine," he had said. "Really. At times like this, I suppose, it's normal to feel like a failure, like everything's falling down around you..." He had stopped himself. "I think we should concentrate on your success. The world opens out for you now, Doctor Trager." He paused. "I want you to know that without working with you, without feeling like I was helping someone else these past months, I'm sure I would have given up entirely. Now, on my life's recent balance sheet there is both profit and loss, where there might only have been loss. Thank you for that." He raised his glass in salute and drank deeply.

After she had left for Washington, he had often thought of her and that night. She had not been fooled by his false gallantry. She knew him too well. He hated himself for having let on. She had a right to be happy.

In the solitude and pointlessness between her departure and Matthew's arrival in the department, Imogen's voice often drifted to him, like a half-remembered scent on the air. The coolness of that voice, its dusky lilt haunted him. He felt sure he was an old fool, sure that dinner the night after her successful defense had not been a missed opportunity at all. Loneliness and desire had misled him fleetingly into believing that she might not, after all, be offended by an advance from him; but he had told himself then, as he told himself now, to put such thoughts away. She was twelve years younger than he, lovely and vital in a way he knew he was not.

At noon, worried she wouldn't call, Calder decided to try another former graduate student. From the back of a drawer he pulled out a business card:

The Washington Post

JERRY INGRAM

Reporter

"City desk," said the man on the other end of the line.

"Good morning," said Calder. "May I speak with Jerry Ingrahm? I thought this was his personal line."

"It is . . . was."

"Was?"

"May I ask who's calling?"

"I'm an old friend, Professor Duncan Calder. He was a student of mine here in Seattle."

"I'm very sorry to tell you, professor, Jerry Ingram died two days ago."

"Oh God. Two days ago?"

"Yes."

"My God...How? What happened?"

"He was involved in a drunk driving accident, professor."

"I'm so sorry," said Calder as he hung up the phone. He stared at the phone on his desk for some moments, not seeing it. Not seeing anything.

The phone rang.

His heart raced. Foreboding swelled in his chest. His back tingled, as though he were sitting facing a fire in a drafty room. He reached slowly for the telephone.

"Professor Calder speaking."

"Hi Duncan, it's Genny." Calder was no longer in a haze. "I just got your message. I'm sorry it took me so long to get back to you. It's been so crazy around here."

"I understand," he said. "Listen, may I call you right back? I have a student here," he lied. "Are you at your office?"

"Yes, I am."

"Good . . . I'll call you right back."

Quickly, he hung up, grabbed his jacket and headed over to the HUB. Calder hoped he could not be monitored from the payphone.

"Genny?" he said when she picked up. "Sorry about that."

"It's okay," she said. "You sounded a bit unsettled. How can I help?"

"I have some information I'd like to show you," he began. "I really can't talk about it on the phone. It turns out that I'll be in Washington tomorrow morning, and I was wondering if you'd care to meet. I'm sure you're busy, but this is very important. Could you spare me an hour or two?"

"Of course, Duncan. Are you okay? You sound odd."

"I'm fine. Really. Where would be a good place to meet?"

"When do you get in?" she asked.

"Pretty early," said Calder. "About six-thirty, your time."

"I'll pick you up."

"I don't want to be any trouble."

"Nonsense. I want to." Imogen did not like the sound of Calder's voice at all. Why couldn't he tell her what all this was about? "We can have breakfast before I go to work, and we can meet again in the evening, if you like. Okay?"

"That sounds perfect, Genny. Thank you." Calder gave her his flight information and thanked her again. "I'm looking forward to seeing you," he said, cringing at the sound of the words, the timbre of his voice, the high school thrill coursing through him despite all the other feelings.

"So am I, Duncan. It's been too long. I'll see you in the morning, then. Good night."

"Good night," said Duncan.

He hung up the phone and went back to his office, his body weak. Matthew dead, Jerry Ingram dead too. If the killers were tapping his phone, they would know he had called the *Post* and found out that Ingram was dead. They would know he was tracing the pattern.

The fatigue of the past few days came showering over him, reducing his limbs, his jaw, his mind, to gelatin. Surely soon all this would be over. Once he'd told Genny all he knew, once he'd shown her the data she could take over. With her connections and aplomb the killings would be stopped.

Duncan sat down and glanced out the window. It was just before 3 p.m., but already the sun had faded. "Good

---

night," he heard Genny say again. Three hours ahead, on the east coast, it was almost night. Here, so far north, under cloud cover that made one doubt the platitudes about the predictability of sunrise, it was almost night, too.

He started as the phone rang again. As he turned to answer, he felt a muscle in his neck spasm and crack, as though someone had snapped their fingers against the side of his neck.

"This is Professor Calder."

"Yes, Mr. Calder. This is Ken at the apartment building."

"Yes?" he said, wondering what the superintendent wanted with him. "Is something wrong?" In his mind, Calder saw the building burning.

"Not really. Only, your son was just here," said Ken, the building manager. "He said you were supposed to be here to give him a letter he needed. It sounded kind of important."

"My son?" repeated Calder. "I don't" He stopped that sentence.

"Yes, and--"

"--You're sure he said he was my son?"

"Yeah, Mark Calder. He showed me his driver's license."

Calder felt his breath coming short. His heart beat rapidly, no longer an undulating muscle but a brittle, metallic toy wound too tightly. He tried to sound calm as he asked, "And did you. . ? Did he find the letter he was looking for?"

"No, sir, he did not. That's what I'm calling about. I'm sorry if you think that was the wrong call, but I didn't know."

"No, no. It's fine. Really. Fine. You did absolutely the right thing."

"I know I did. It's not just building policy," said Fitzwilliam. "Policy I might bend. But that's the U.S. Mail."

"Thank you."

"Anyway, he left before I could call you. But I thought I

should do it anyway. Once before something like this happened, the parents of the kid called up my supervisor, the owner of the building, saying I'd been discourteous."

"Ken...Mr...?

"Fitzwilliam."

"Mr Fitzwilliam. Thank you. You did absolutely right. I apologize for putting you in that situation." Calder hung up.

Calder's brain was now firing on all cylinders, but unfortunately, the car was in neutral. Should he have told Fitzwilliam he didn't have a son? Had that been a test? He wouldn't have known Fitzwilliam's voice on the telephone. Maybe they were calling with this scenario figuring that if he knew nothing, he would tell the truth; and now that he had remained silent about not having any children, they would know he knew something. Maybe they were testing his reaction. Maybe they now planned on breaking into his mailbox. In any case, they knew about the copied data.

Duncan rolled slightly back from his desk, the casters of his chair making a scratching sound on the wood floor. He looked under his desk. Nothing. He got down on his knees, and reached under the desk. He patted behind the back of the center drawer, his fingers aching to touch paper but finding only the cold steel of the desk.

CHAPTER NINE

December 14, 2016

Calder felt a cold rush of nausea fill him as he crouched on the floor behind his desk. He rose to his feet and fell back into his chair. His hands trembled as he opened his email account and typed in the password. He would have to get the information to Genny immediately. It was the only thing that might save him.

The screen flashed "incorrect user name or password" in red letters.

He swallowed hard, which only accentuated the cold, bitter sickness rising within him. He removed the thumbdrive from his pocket, preparing to plug it in. He told himself to calm down, that he couldn't afford to make mistakes. He threw his head back, took a deep breath and started typing his password again.

"Incorrect user name or password." Calder typed it a third time, much more slowly. He checked that he didn't have 'caps lock' on, checked that his user name was correct and hit return. "Incorrect user name or password."

He stared at the blinking cursor.

Then grabbed his keys, his coat and rushed out of his office. He walked quickly along one of the main paths across the Quad, not knowing where he was going. He felt defeated, foolish, sick with fear.

On one of the benches near the Art building, he sat down. He scanned the Quad for anyone following him, but no one looked suspicious or out of place. Even if he couldn't see the enemy, he knew they were near. He couldn't go home, couldn't stay in his office. It seemed safest to stay in public, he felt, but he probably shouldn't stay in one place for long.

So far, every death they had perpetrated had looked like an accident. Was there anything in that to help him? he wondered. He hoped that it meant they wouldn't just shoot him. Someone could walk up to him and threaten him with a gun, but would they really shoot him?

Calder walked to University Way, the main drag, as the rain fell more and more heavily. He stopped at the most public cash machine he could find and withdrew $500, as much as he could at any one time. His chest was still tight with fear, but he felt oddly free—he had cash, he didn't need any bags and he could pick up his ticket at the airport. But his flight didn't leave for almost four hours.

Calder looked up and down University Way for somewhere to stay warm for a few hours. A pub nearby looked perfect. It had windows all round and was bright and nearly empty. The pub's emptiness, which other nights had caused him to reject it as a place to drink, suddenly seemed its greatest recommendation: open, public, but not crowded, he should be safe there. As he walked down the block toward the pub, the rain began to fall in torrents.

The pub was warm, clean and well lighted. Had the wood of the bar and back bar not been antique, deeply stained oak, there would have been no charm at all to the place. It would have seemed garishly bright and antiseptic. As it was, though, it felt lived in, comfortable. A few paintings covered the walls opposite the bar.

Duncan felt utterly pointless, stateless. His home was not safe, his office was not safe. He studied the wines on the pub's special board and ordered a Ken Wright Cellars Oregon Pinot Noir. The wine was precisely what he needed, big, elegant; bold but with a depth of fruit. The wine flowing down his throat warmed him from the inside. He shivered momentarily, dispelling the chill from under his wet clothes.

Things might work out, he thought.

As he took in his surroundings, he began imagining how his enemy—as he now thought of the nameless murders— might deal with him here. His heart sank. He was sitting in practically the worst place in the bar. People on the street could see all the way to the back, which would make abduction problematic, but on the other hand the room was long and narrow which would make it hard for him to escape. Though the ceilings were high and the mirror behind the bar made the room feel bigger, he couldn't shake the feeling that it was shrinking around him.

During the past few days, for the first time in his life, he had been forced to contemplate the security of his surroundings. The people who designed offices, apartments and public spaces seemed to count too much on the beneficence of others, on the stability of society, he concluded—and for him, there was no longer any such stability. He stood up, collected his things and walked to the front booth, from which he might have a chance of escaping. The bartender watched him for a moment impassively, and then returned to his cleaning.

Calder twisted in his seat slightly so that he faced toward the door, took out a writing pad and began taking mental stock of what he knew, and what he thought was going on. "Seven Electors are dead," he said to himself "and all of them belonged to the Democratic Party. Each of the seven died in a state where there was a Democratic plurality. Okay, I think I can prove to Genny that we can rule out coincidence; that this is statistically significant. So: why is this happening? Why have these Electors been killed? What is gained by it? and who are the people doing it?" Although he had written nothing down, having the notepad out somehow helped him to clarify his thoughts.

"Okay," he thought, "what if these seven replacements are plants? It seems logical. Kill off the Elector, and replace him or her with a Faithless Elector." He nodded to himself as much to say: "Yes, that's presumably what they're up to."

But this didn't answer all the questions. "Why seven? Christopher lost to Redmond by four Electoral votes. Since all any candidate needs is a simple majority of Electoral votes, the conspirators would only need to replace three Electors to change the Presidency. Why seven?" He signaled for another glass of wine.

"Margin for error? Perhaps they can't count on all of the replacements to be Faithless. After all, how can you trust someone who agrees to compromise a Presidential election?"

What most impressed Calder but also rankled the most was that these people had chosen the weakest point in the electoral process. They were relying on the apathy and ignorance of the citizens. At precisely the time when no one thought to look at what was going on—indeed when most thought the election was already settled—a small group had struck at the very heart of the process. If Matthew hadn't checked out the data he had come across by chance, they would have got away with it. Matthew had paid with his life, and they still might get away with it. The integrity of the nation was in Calder's hands.

Fear ebbed slightly, as he was overwhelmed by indignation at the hubris of the criminals and anger at Matthew's death. Politics was a dirty pursuit, of course. Everyone knew that politicians twist the truth even when they are not telling outright lies. But this was not some cynical exchange of rhetoric and trumped up statistics to do with denying unemployment assistance in favor of funding something else; it was not about gutting environmental law for private gain. Those debates, however full of trickery and spin, were nevertheless just that—debates—and they were more or less overt, carried out before the public and in the public's name.

This plot, though, was covert, a nationally organized

93

threat to the integrity of the office of the President. It was secret, precise in its economy, and deadly in pursuit of its goal. If the plot succeeded, the government would not legitimately derive its "just powers from the consent of the governed."

Calder had spent more than twenty years studying and teaching about elections; and while his primary interest was academic, and despite his stated ambivalence about the "real world," that theory and practice was underpinned by an abiding, visceral connection to what was it was all for—people: their rights, their lives and livelihoods; the just and lawful application and use of power. He found himself filled with outrage.

He wondered again about who the conspirators were. That it involved Republicans or the Republican Party was certain; the Democrats had nothing to gain and everything to lose. Calder couldn't see the Republican Party leadership doing something like this. It was too risky, far beyond the normal kinds of "dirty tricks" a party would be likely to countenance. Did they know at the top level, like Watergate, and so would neither help nor hinder the conspirators? Or had some private, well-heeled and well-connected set of ideologues seen this dirty plot as a means to get their way, abetted by the confusion wealth in American politics affords?

Hours later, Calder was no nearer figuring out who was doing the killing and manipulation than when he sat down. Finally, he asked the bartender to call a taxi for him.

The rain still fell in thick droplets. When the taxi arrived, the driver merely honked for Calder to get inside the car. The windows instantly fogged up as he flung himself on the back seat. He quickly scooted to the side opposite the driver, who had rolled down his window in order to see.

"Airport," said Calder. The driver nodded and cut across University Way, over a double-yellow line, through a parking lot and alley and onto 15th Street. The taxi had no side-view mirrors, so as he drove, the cabbie occupied himself by alternately pounding on the dashboard in a vain attempt to get the defroster to work better, and craning his neck out the window elaborately every minute or so to see to the side and behind. Calder's life was threatened not only by a sinister conspiracy but by a maniac in charge of a potentially lethal taxi. As they careened up the street at high speed, the driver was thumping the dashboard and wiping the windshield with his fist when at the last moment he would see a parked truck right in front of him, crane out the window, change lanes, pass the truck and veer back to his original lane; by this time, the windshield had fogged over, so he would bang, wipe, lean and risk their lives again.

There were few cars out by this hour, and fewer pedestrians, which was just as well. Calder both dreaded and was grateful for the rain which kept everyone else inside, since the likelihood of hitting something or someone increased in direct proportion to the number of chances of doing so. Weak and powerless in the back seat, he tried to be calm : "I'm in no hurry," he said, to no effect; then "Wasn't that a red light?" he said as the car turned and hurtled along 45th Street.

He detected a slight curving of the shoulders in the cab driver, a menacing stoop to his neck. "Do you have a job?" the man asked, looking at him in the inside rearview mirror.

"Yes."

"Do I tell you how to do it?"

"I. I wasn't telling you how to do your job . . . just—"

"—Kibitzing," the driver interjected.

"Kibitzing?"

"Kibitzing," the cabby pronounced. "It applies no matter what your intent."

Calder paused, and then began firmly: "My intent"

"Doesn't matter because the result is the same: whether you think you can do this job better than I is not at issue.

Though we know the truth of that, don't we? I mean, if you were as good at this as I am, you'd be paid to do it, wouldn't you? Nevertheless, you are looking over my shoulder and attempting to offer advice—kibitzing."

"Kibitzing."

"I'm glad we understand one another," said the driver.

Calder nodded slowly. Though he wasn't at all sure they understood one another, he was reluctant to prolong the conversation by voicing further reservations. To make matters worse, he could think of no way to begin objecting without sounding like some pompous character from a Victorian novel, who might begin, "Now listen here, my good man."

But now the ice was broken, the driver's thoughts flowed rapidly. "See, here's the thing: you're okay. I can tell. But a lot of people—other people—a lot of people right now would be asking me my name so they could report me to my supervisor because 1 wasn't properly docile and compliant in the face of their insults. A lot of people, they take this whole 'service economy' thing way too literally. They think we're all supposed to be servants, rather than providing service.

"Service is noble. It is. This country could do with a little more of a sense of obligation and service to others. But at the moment it's buried in greed and a perversion of the service ethic, so instead of being ennobled by serving others, the people who work for their living like me feel so shit on by the so-called higher-ups (whether we admit it to ourselves or not) that we turn around and shit on everyone else whenever we perceive ourselves as in a position of advantage. You know?"

Calder, bewildered, decided that discretion was the better part of valor at the moment and only nodded.

"So, here's the thing: right now, our relation to one another is that I am the highly skilled and knowledgeable technician who knows these roads like the back of his hand,

and you are the client who needs the service I am providing, for reasons it is not necessarily my business to know. But while you are in my cab, you accept the service from me, and I am the captain of my ship."

As he spoke, he continued his weaving in and out of traffic. Had he not been quite so occupied with dodging other cars, and had the rear window not been so fogged up, or had there been side-view mirrors, he might have noticed that another car was following his erratic path through the city toward the freeway, leaping forward around cars as the taxi did and settling into lanes whenever the taxi did.

As the cab neared the ramp to the freeway, the driver suddenly interrupted himself, stepped on the brake, threw the wheel the opposite direction and accelerated down a side-street. He quickly recovered the car from a violent fishtail. "There must be an accident on I-5," he said. "Look back at those cars. They're standing still."

Calder did as he was told, and as he looked behind, he saw a dark blue car slide sideways around the corner after them. It recovered as well and as quickly as the cab driver had.

"He's almost as good as you," said Calder, checking the tightness of his seatbelt.

"Who?" asked the driver.

"That blue car behind you."

The cabby craned his head backward. His eyes narrowed briefly as he looked at the car. "We'll take highway ninety-nine to the airport instead," said the driver as he returned his attention to the road ahead of him. Calder nodded, making eye contact with the driver in the rearview mirror. The driver held his gaze on Calder a little longer than seemed necessary, as though the driver were sizing him up again.

"What do you do for work?" asked the driver. "We've talked about me—what about you?"

"Not much to tell, really," Calder replied. "I'm a

professor of Political Science at the university."

"No shit?" said the driver. "That was my major."

Duncan smiled, his heart sinking at the prospect of having something in common with the driver.

"What's your specialty, professor?"

"American Government."

"American Government," the driver repeated. "I mostly did theory . . . actually, I never really had a major. I just took classes I liked for about four years. Read a lot."

"Sounds fun," said Calder.

"I enjoyed it. Didn't get a degree, but I don't really need one, now do I?"

"You would be the best judge of that," said Calder.

The driver turned around and smiled.

"Listen," he said after a moment. "I'm going to give you a flat rate to the airport—forty-two dollars. I'm going to keep the meter running, and you pay whichever is cheaper."

"Sounds fair," Calder replied.

"It is fair," said the driver. "And by the way, we're not going to take the Viaduct south. Scares me to death. You remember the 'eighty-nine earthquake in Northern California right during the World Series?"

Calder nodded.

"Remember that bridge over to Oakland or Berkley? that two-tier job? that picture of the car falling through? That's what'll happen here in the next big quake we have. Only it'll be worse.

"Do you know the term 'liquefaction'?" the driver asked as the car bottomed out across a side street and then seemed to bounce off the ground as it continued downhill. "It happens when the water in the earth rises suddenly in an earthquake, turning the ground to jelly. It happens in soil that has no rock in it. Nothing built on that kind of soil will stand in an earthquake. That's pure landfill the Viaduct's built on. Dirt. Deep, deep, dirt with a lot of water in it. That's all.

"The thing—the Viaduct—it won't just fall over on its side the way those overpasses in Kobe, Japan did either. It'll break into a million pieces."

Did he really not understand, Calder found himself wondering, that the probability of the driver being killed in an accident was far greater than the probability of him dying on a bridge in an earthquake—particularly given the crazy way he drove.

"I know what you're thinking," said the driver, "and I suppose you're right. You think if I drove a bit less aggressively, I would further reduce my chances of being killed, and that being afraid of the minute chance I might be on the viaduct at the moment an earthquake hit is silly. Am I wrong?"

"You know," said Calder, smiling despite himself, "I usually hate it when people tell me they know what I'm thinking 'cause they're always wrong. But you're right: that's exactly what I was thinking."

The driver smiled again. "Anyway, professor," he continued, "I'm afraid pure rationale can't work here. See, this is about control. I can control the direction of the car, its speed. I know what it can do and what it cannot do. I cannot control other drivers, but I can somewhat predict their behavior based on past experience. I cannot control an earthquake, so I control what I can and stay off that damn death-trap."

"I'd call that rational enough," said Calder.

"I take that as a compliment." The driver flexed his hands and resettled himself in his seat, ready for the bridge grate he was about to pass over. Five lanes of traffic traversed the First Avenue South drawbridge over the Duwamish Waterway, two north, two south, and one "reversible," closed to both directions now that rush hour was over.

In the heavy rain, the bridge grate, despite the city's

repeated efforts to make it safer, would be slick. The tires of each car had to remain on the less slippery safety coating laid down like white tracks across the metal grating or the tires would slip as though on ice. It was particularly important to remain on the "tracks" as there was an abrupt curve in the bridge at its crest. As the taxi curved toward the drawbridge, the driver happened to glance to his right where he noticed the headlights go off on the dark blue car behind him.

As the wheels of the taxi hit the safety strips, the driver lost sight of the blue car as it dipped behind and further to the right of him, changing lanes in an area where road signs gave repeated prohibitions against lane changes. The blue car was now in the blind spot created by the fogging over of Calder's window and the rear window. Though he was approaching the turn on the bridge, the point that even he would normally take slowly, the driver, as if by instinct, accelerated.

His instinct had been good, but a moment too late. As the car approached the top of the bridge, about to curve to the right, the expected inertial tug of the turn was suddenly not a gentle tug but a crunch, and the car did not curve right, but began to slide sideways to the left as the blue car slammed into the taxi.

"Son of a bitch," hissed the driver and stomped on the accelerator. The car was about to come out of the slide when the blue car suddenly smashed it again on the forward passenger-side door. The back-end swung wide. The taxi began sliding across the empty reversible lane and into the lanes of oncoming traffic. Horns blared all around.

Impotent in the back seat, Calder experienced everything as though in slow motion, the car's skid, the slight feeling of weightlessness, like they were going over the edge of something. He saw the aggression of the blue car, the sparks arcing between the two vehicles. He became focused on the driver, his only hope. The driver had been right. He was very good at his job. Calder had seen the myriad tiny corrections he had made so far to keep going, and for a moment he thought they would make it.

A second later, though, with the taxi now turned sideways, he saw the approaching metal lane barrier, where the southbound lanes jogged right again to meet up with Highway 590. The barrier jutted out from the south end of the bridge like a wedge to split the traffic, and the point of the wedge was aiming directly at Calder.

The taxi had now passed over the crest of the bridge and they were both looking downward. Calder inhaled deeply, resigned to the coming impact, when the driver yelled "Got it!"

In an instant, the driver was no longer attempting to hold out against the blue car, fighting to regain the southbound lane. He had accelerated again and turned to the left. The engine gave a piercing whine as Calder felt the taxi come out of the slide and dive into the oncoming traffic. The blue car, now lacking force against its left side, spun wildly sideways, driving its own passenger side into the barrier, where the car buckled, wrapping itself around the wedge.

The taxi driver leaned on his horn as the taxi slalomed through the northbound traffic. Other cars swerved round them, honking furiously. For a moment, the taxi ran right down the center of the two oncoming lanes, the headlights of the oncoming traffic strobing through the inside of the cab. The driver picked a slight break in the traffic and darted over to the shoulder. Less than an eighth of a mile from the bridge, the driver crept down an on-ramp, traversed the road and stopped in a gravel turnout.

The driver unhooked his hands from the steering wheel and stared at them. Calder looked at himself as though he might be missing integral parts. It was moments later that he thought to remove his hand from the door handle he had been clutching.

The driver got out and examined the car. Calder

wondered whether he should get out of this car which has so nearly killed him, or whether it was his only protection. Did he want to continue the journey? Go to D.C. for his meeting with Genny, or wait here by the roadside until the police turned up? He felt paralyzed. As he was trying to calm down and think, the driver hopped back into the car. "No real damage, mostly cosmetic," he said. "Tell me, professor, are you like a really unfair grader?""

Calder laughed, and as he did so, he realized he hadn't laughed in days, had felt no release from the anxieties he'd been through. The driver began laughing, too.

"No," said Calder, suddenly feeling the weight of his secret again. "The guy was probably just crazy."

"Yeah. I guess I really pissed somebody off."

"It was a nice piece of driving."

"Thank you," said the driver. He stared at the steering wheel. "The airport, huh?"

"If you're okay."

The driver shrugged.

They drove in silence for a moment or two as the driver glided uncharacteristically slow along the small highway.

"I think they really wanted to kill us, didn't they?" said the cab driver suddenly. He looked back at Calder in the rearview mirror.

"It sure seemed like it," Calder allowed.

"Damn," said the driver, shivering. He fell silent again. Then: "I'll tell you, though: it focuses the mind, doesn't it? Everything was going slow motion for me."

"Me, too," said Calder.

"It's like a survival technique. Like how we use only three per cent of our brain's capacity or whatever? only maybe to avoid death, some hormone kicks in and boosts that capacity. You're in danger and you're working and thinking, trying to find a way out, and you feel like you've got all the time in the world. That car was driving me sideways. I could feel the back-end breaking loose, and for a moment it was like a puzzle. I was detached, like 'hmm . . . how am I going to do this?' Because I knew: I knew I would get out of it."

Calder smiled, exhaled.

"When I saw that break, saw how much space there was between the cars in the oncoming lane . . . I've never felt anything so pure."

"You yelled 'I got it'," said Calder.

"Is that what I said?" Calder could see him smile in the mirror as he shook his head. "It was. It was perfect . . . and to leave that motherfucker wrapped up like that . . . still, perfect." He chuckled to himself. "Anyway," he said, noticing the money Calder was proffering, and only then realizing that they were at the airport.

He helped Calder out of the back.

"Stay safe, professor," he said as he discreetly spread the bills Duncan had given him into a fan to count the money.

"They'll be here, too," thought Duncan as the sliding glass doors to the Seattle-Tacoma International Airport jumped apart. "Christ," he thought as he walked along, trying not to reveal that he was weighing up the malicious intent of every passerby, "how do criminals do it? How do they live so long being hunted?"

With just over an hour until the plane left, Duncan considered his options. The more public the place, he decided, the better. Calder glanced up at a television screen which gave departure times and gates. As he stood there, he suddenly wondered if "they" knew where he was going and on which flight?

He stood as though mesmerized by the information while he tried to think of what to do next. There was a seat right next to the the bank of television monitors. "Public," thought Calder, "and completely open." He sat down.

"Okay," he thought. "It's possible they only figured out I

was going somewhere when I got in the cab. If that is the case, I need to keep them guessing. Stay in the open."

Duncan approved of the airport's design, wide, spacious, unlike most of the places in which he had found himself lately. He could not relax, but he could worry less.

And yet, it was an airport. Calder, from his vantage point beneath the arrival and departure monitors, was touched by its strangeness. People moved about quickly, some frantically. Only a very few were not in motion, and those few seemed perfectly at home within their inertia, as though resting in preparation for something momentous. A great many of his fellow travellers were on cell phones, which served only to increase his paranoia. The floor gleamed. The whole place was kept at a high, sterile gloss, as though no one ever walked on the floor, as though dirt had to be left outside, like pets.

An automatic subway train served the satellites where the departure gates were clustered. The expressions of the people passing down the escalator toward it were bovine in their dull impatience. "Not one of them knows," he thought.

Calder felt sick and alone. The only people who looked comfortable, as though they belonged, were the police, who lounged across railings and talked on their radios. Once again fear that the police—at a much higher level than these guys—might be part of the conspiracy surfaced in Duncan's mind.

"Okay," he thought, "So far, all their killings have been made to look like accidents. If they murder me here, it will not look like an accident. Even a random robbery and killing would be suspicious. Even if they have bugged my phone, they can't know what I may have told colleagues, people who might make connections if I were to turn up murdered after Matthew's accident.

"They could put a bomb on the plane!" thought Calder suddenly. "No," he thought, calming himself. "That would definitely draw attention. If their operating procedure remains constant, they won't do anything that draws national attention. I have to stay in the open until the flight leaves."

He scanned the multitude, looking for anything out of place, anyone who was looking at him. He wanted a drink but decided against it. He would need all his faculties to remain alive long enough to get on the plane. Yet the allure of a clean, crisp whiskey was difficult to shake.

He looked again at the monitors announcing departures. He should get his ticket, he thought. Four flights by the same airline were leaving within 45 minutes of each other, all from gates on "N" Satellite.

He stood up, but as he did so, he noticed a man a few rows away from where he was sitting put down his paper and stand up. Calder sat down. His heart beat quickly.

"I could go to a random gate," he thought, "throw him off the trail."

At that moment, he noticed a small sign in the hallway above the escalator: "No admittance to gates without a boarding pass." His heart leapt. He might be safe at the "N" Satellite. He walked toward check in.

As he approached the queue, his heart knocked frantically. He thought of scenarios in which someone would get behind in line him with a gun, drive the barrel into his back ribs, whispering quietly for him to come away, and he would be dead before the car left the airport garage.

Rather than walk directly to the ticket counter line, he dawdled, stopping to examine a newspaper someone had left, again to check the departure monitors of another airline, and again to pretend to check that his watch was still working. Each time, just before going on, he would look for someone behind who had also stopped moving.

Duncan approached the ticket counter. He joined the serpentine queue and glanced around. He did not like the look of the man who quickly entered behind him (blonde, beefy, immaculately groomed); so he pretended there was something in his pockets he had to look for, and waved the man past: "Please. Go ahead. Sorry."

As Calder left the ticket counter, his boarding pass stuffed into the breast pocket of his blazer, a crushing thought hit him: the killers did not need to know which flight he was on in order to buy any ticket at random and follow him out to the gate. It was important to keep them guessing.

As he wound his way toward the escalator, Calder noticed the same beefy man from the queue walking his direction. When their eyes made contact, the man had the casually penetrating gaze of a cop, the air of entitlement of those who belong.

Calder began his descent on the escalator. Beefy was a few steps above him. At the bottom, Calder turned left and got into line to be screened. Everyone had boarding passes at the ready. A few people stood off to the side, saying farewells. Calder's body felt electric, charged, as though it might arc if touched. He stole a backward glance at Beefy, three behind him in the queue. In his mind, he was already jumping at the firm but gentle touch on his shoulder, recoiling from the voice which asked him to step out of line please and keep quiet.

As Calder looked back again, Beefy was walking forward. Calder instantly turned around to face away. As he came within his peripheral view, Calder felt violently sick. As Beefy walked past, Calder had seen where his blazer bulged to show the service revolver holstered under the arm. As the man came even with Duncan, he pointed at one of the security guards and then off toward a corner of the room past the security checkpoint. The security guard nodded, picked up a checklist of some sort and walked to meet him. He held up a wide identity card as he bypassed the checkpoint.

Calder walked through the metal detector. Beefy and the guard conferred over some point on the checklist, ignoring him entirely. As he waited for the train to take him to the satellite, he looked back again at the security guard and Beefy in his smart blazer, still in conference. It had been a false alarm. He sighed and drew a deep breath.

The train arrived and the doors split, disgorging passengers. Calder waited a moment and then entered. He sat down on one of the benches, exhausted, and put his face in his hands. The recorded safety messages in Japanese, Chinese and English were equally indifferent to him. He could not think, could not decide what to do. English sounded as foreign as Japanese. He raised his face from his hands and looked about blankly. Any one of his fellow passengers could have been planted there, he thought distantly.

Though it would be days before he could fully articulate the change in him, he had glimpsed something of the truth in what the taxi driver had said about the workings of the mind. The calmness that takes hold in difficult situations was not, he decided, the body's way of preparing for death. It was about focus, about screening out all extraneous noises and thoughts and finding a way out. The animal that is run to exhaustion turns on its pursuers not because of the nobility of going down fighting but because its best bet—flight—has failed, so now its best hope of remaining alive is attack.

Calder had always prided himself on his ability to take in all data relevant to a given problem, being exhaustive in gathering all that was relevant and coming out with a synthesis. But his conclusions came slowly, as the result of reflection, deliberately and in the fullness of time. That way of thinking was no use now. It might be once again, if he survived, but for now, he needed to act.

The "whys" regarding the murder of Matthew and the seven Electors were no longer as important as the certainty that they had happened, and that someone was out to kill him as well. There was a single object in his mind: not to give away what flight he was getting on. That the killers might already know where he was going did not occur to him.

As the double-doors spread at the 'N' Satellite and Calder got off, he was no longer frightened, no longer even concerned. They were there, or they were not there. He was being followed, or he was not being followed. Calder walked off the train and got into the queue with the others, single-file up the escalator. He looked neither ahead nor behind.

The "N" Satellite at the Seattle-Tacoma International Airport was a large square, with the departure gates situated all around the outside. In the center there was a bar, coffee shop, gift shop, newsstand and bathrooms. Calder's plane would leave from Gate N-4, directly ahead of him as he stepped off the escalator. Instead of walking to it, he turned right with most of the other passengers. He went to the newsstand and bought a *New York Times*, "Justice Department to begin Tampering Investigation," read the headline. Then he went to the bathroom.

He checked the narrow hallway before entering, and, seeing that no one was coming, went inside. The bathroom was long and narrow. The urinals were parallel with the hallway. The stalls were along the opposite wall. The sinks were to his right, just past the entry. He was alone in the bathroom.

As he glanced over his shoulder to his right, watching for anyone coming in, he heard a door creak open, and quickly looked left. There were two entryways. Calder looked briefly at who was coming in, and then looked right, wondering if they might try some pincer maneuver. But no one came in the door on the right side. Calder zipped his trousers quickly and walked out.

It occurred to him, if he was supposed to be killed on the way to the airport, there might not be anyone there to watch him. Perhaps they hadn't allowed for the possibility that he might make it this far.

Though his plane left from N-4, Calder walked to N-12, on the opposite side of the square but in view of N-4 to sit and wait. The plane leaving N-12 for Chicago departed only ten minutes after his own.

As Calder sat with some of the other passengers, he noticed two men walking next to each other but not talking. There would have been no reason to suppose they were together except that they looked similar, mid-twenties and clean-cut, like initiates recently graduated from some evangelical youth group, tentative yet arrogant. These two, one with dark hair, the other with hair so fine it shone like white gold under the fluorescent lamps, looked very much like people Calder might have found before him in a Junior level course. Yet he found himself gazing at them a little longer than at any of the other passengers. But then they separated, one heading for N12, the other for N-13.

Neither young man carried any luggage. As Calder stole a glance over his newspaper at the dark-haired man, Calder noticed he was staring at the blond man before he felt Calder's eyes on him. He met Calder's gaze momentarily, then averted his eyes to the floor. He bit his lip sullenly, forcing himself not to look up again. Calder had to restrain himself too, so as not to smile at the young man's clumsiness. He had never until that moment been able to identify someone following or watching him. Any of the others who might have been tailing him had been more discreet.

But how could he lose them? Calder did not think about what he would do but simply stood up. Directly in front of him was a bar. He looked at his watch, shrugged and walked into the lounge. As he leaned on the bar, he heard the first call for his flight to Washington D.C., momentarily cutting off the droning piped music, which was all the more cloying for being relentless Christmas Muzak. Calder had two Scotches in rapid succession as he listened for the next boarding call. He was ordering a third as "Santa Claus is Coming to Town" was interrupted for a call to Gate 12, "with service to Chicago."

Calder looked out toward the gates. He gulped the drink. Within the burning rush created by the whiskey there came a clarity. He would get rid of them. He saw the young man sitting at Gate 12 begin to fidget.

Calder glanced across at his own flight. The line was getting shorter. The main call for the flight to Chicago was immediately followed by the second call for all passengers to board at N-4. Calder began making an elaborate show of leaving. He noticed the young man at Gate 13 snap from his daydream. As he did so, the other came to life, though what they had in mind for him, he did not know. Calder paid and left the bar, not toward either gate, but away.

His flight now began calling individual names of people he guessed were standby passengers. He did not look back, but he slowed his pace. He was walking too quickly. He forced a deep breath, paused and glanced at his watch. Turning toward the bathrooms, he saw out of the corner of his eye that both men following him. He turned down the hallway to the bathrooms.

Instead of walking into the men's room, Calder walked into the ladies'. He paused just inside the door, grateful he was alone. Calder stood still, hoping for a host of reasons that no one came in. He listened, holding his breath, his ears aching to hear the door to the men's room open.

He heard it. Calder waited another moment, and then bolted down the hallway from which he had come. There was one standby passenger left at the desk, but Calder was not about to allow his seat to be taken. As he ran, he grabbed the ticket from his inside breast pocket like a fistful of dollars and began waving it. The ticket agent noticed him and stood back from the customer at the counter.

As he arrived at the top of the gangway, the ticket agent

gave him a brief up-and-down look, and then took his ticket. Calder ran down the gangway, but stopped running as he reached the bend where it met the door of the aircraft. Just before he turned to step aboard, he saw the two eager young men back in the satellite, sprinting toward Gate 12.

CHAPTER TEN

December 15, 2016

Imogen had arrived early to meet Duncan's flight. She parked two car lengths behind the last taxi in the taxi lane, which, though illegal, she felt was a judicious and fair place to park: it was free and she was not blocking anyone's access to their trade. And what could they do? If they told her to move along, she would drive round the loop past the passenger pickup area, a circuit which took no more than three or four minutes. Since there was only one flight arriving from Seattle at Dulles Airport at 6:45 a.m., she was pretty sure she could find the gate, and she thought momentarily about parking and going in to wait for Calder there, but she decided against it.

Glancing at the clock on her dashboard as she waited behind the cabs, Imogen could no longer pretend to herself that she was early simply because she had misjudged the time it took to get to the airport. It was more. Despite how strange he had sounded, she was excited to see Duncan. She was eager to talk with him, to impress him. She hoped he would have time to come by her office to see what she was doing. He might be very interested in her work on the Illinois election returns. She hoped they might relax over dinner, and had been thinking of places she might take him.

She settled back in the driver's seat and began reviewing some papers about the Illinois returns. She had all the data lined up, and would get to work as soon as she had dropped Duncan at his hotel. It was possible she would have an answer for Pollack at the end of the day. As she read, she absently reached for her coffee cup, perched on top of her briefcase in the passenger seat. As she did so, lifting it delicately to her lips, she looked around. In the half hour since she had arrived, activity around Dulles Airport had increased dramatically.

It was ten minutes until Duncan's flight touched down, assuming it was on time, twenty or twenty-five minutes more before he would be coming out. Imogen took a long sip from her coffee cup, relaxing into the warmth flooding down through her body. It was a cold day. The sun was shining, but the air was below freezing, as the snow heaped on either side of the road attested. Imogen took another sip, enjoying the sensation of being warm within such cold. She was wondering how it was that she could drink coffee too hot to hold, even though her lips and mouth were far more sensitive than her hands, when a policeman rapped on the window.

"Yes?" she asked as she rolled down her window, enjoying the pretense that she didn't know full well why he wanted to talk with her.

"You can't park here, ma'am."

"I can't?"

"No. You can't."

"I'm terribly sorry, officer. I didn't know. I'm waiting to pick someone up . . ."

"Uh huh. So is just about everyone else, and I don't let any of them park along here either. Move along."

Imogen drained the last of her coffee, put away her papers and started the engine. She unlocked the passenger door, though by her reckoning, it was still at least twenty minutes until Duncan would be outside, which meant at least six circuits. She promised herself she wouldn't begin looking for him until she had made five round trips.

Duncan had not slept a moment on the plane, and he was beginning to feel himself slip. The eerie sensation he had felt some days earlier when he had stayed up all night had returned. Colors again seemed more vibrant, hard objects again looked porous. He found himself doubting his mastery of language. As the descent began, the stewardess had said something to him, and he had replied, but now, as the jet settled into its final approach, he could not remember what they had said, or for that matter if he had said anything at all.

Even so, as the plane descended over the Virginia countryside he felt like a man who has been marooned on an island when he sees a ship steaming toward him. Having had only unspoken thoughts as his companions, he might find it overwhelming at first to be able to speak freely to someone else—but to speak would be his rescue.

The landing gear opened beneath him. His ears popped, and in the same instant he lost the momentary feeling of relief. His excitement about seeing Genny had more than a tincture of dread, because of the danger he might be involving her in, despite his best efforts to shield her. He must assume there would be someone at the gate and someone who would tail them through Washington. They would want to know who he had spoken to and what that other person knew before killing them both.

Calder felt he needed a plan. He thought he remembered her car, a silver Honda Accord. There were many such cars on the road, which was both good and bad, he thought. As it was a common car, there was also the danger he would pick the wrong one and tip his hand too early.

The plane docked and Calder stood up. He collected his jacket from the overhead locker. He took a deep breath, as though preparing to sprint through the terminal. Nevertheless, he walked slowly through the terminal, trying to see the best way forward.

A line of people were ambling toward the taxi stand outside. Calder saw them as providing cover and safety for him, and he drifted toward the taxi line. As he stepped out of the airport into the cold December air, he took quick stock of his surroundings. There seemed to be about twelve or fifteen people in the taxi line ahead of him. Thus far, he had made no attempt to figure out if anyone was following him; but as he slowed his pace to get in line, he heard a man walking up quickly behind, his steps rapping sharply across the sidewalk. Calder stopped and turned to look, his heart beating rapidly. As he turned, he began patting his coat as though he had misplaced something important. "Go ahead," Calder said politely to the man and got into the queue behind him.

In the Seattle-Tacoma airport Duncan had found himself sneering at the thought and effort that went into packaging human beings just to get them from place to place. He had found himself particularly sickened by the glum, bovine acceptance of it all by his fellow travelers. Here, waiting for a taxi, it was no different: two lines converged at right angles. A taxi pulled up, the person at the front of the line got in, the taxi drove off, and the process was repeated, beginning the next stage in shipment of the package. The container ship had docked and was disgorging its contents onto trains and waiting semis which would take the products to their various destinations.

It was clear, dry and cold, with the sun glaring and dazzling on the low piles of snow at the side of the road. Calder blinked and squinted in the abundance of light. Beyond the single-file taxi-only lane, separated by a traffic island, the main road had four more lanes for pick up and drop-off. Calder scanned the lanes for Imogen's car. He thought he saw it drive past. It had slowed momentarily, as though the driver were looking at the traffic island where Calder should have been standing. Presumably she would keep driving round, but he felt he shouldn't make his move yet. Anyone following must be made to believe that he was about to take a cab.

He checked his watch, and when the car came round again, he saw Imogen's unmistakable profile and a brassy flash of red hair inside the car. The circuit had taken her three minutes, and there were still eight people in front of him in the line. As casually as he could, he examined them. No one was obviously watching him or waiting to follow. What about cars? He scanned the road beyond the traffic island, which was full of cars letting people on and off but saw nothing remarkable.

His strategy had been to remain in public as much as possible. It would be much harder, he thought, to take him out of a line waiting for the taxi than if he had stood on the traffic island to wait for a ride, where they would simply drive up to him, point a gun and tell him to get in. Calder hoped the enemy was poised to follow the cab he appeared to be waiting for. Traffic was growing thicker with people picking up and dropping off. In the confusion, he might get away with something of a head start.

It was two minutes before Imogen's car would reappear around the corner. Calder was fourth in line for a cab. He hated airports. It was no good scanning for people who looked suspicious, or too clean cut, or who talked on handheld radios. There were lots of each. Now he was third in line. His heart beat frantically as he reached the front of the line. Suddenly, he saw Imogen's car.

She was growing impatient. This was no way to go about picking people up, she thought. Too haphazard. For twenty minutes now she had been constantly changing lanes, honking at people, trying to keep an eye out for Duncan while staying aware of very unpredictable traffic. If Calder ever again uttered the words "don't want to be any trouble", she would explain to him how the world worked outside the confines of a university. She slowed as she approached the terminal's pick-up area and looked for Calder.

Calder was aware of an unnatural silence as he prepared to run. Across the wide concrete expanse, he saw both the next cab to his left in the taxi-only lane, and, in the outer lanes, Imogen's car coming up quickly. He couldn't be sure—would never be sure—but he also thought he saw a man who had been standing by the curb climb into a blue Ford. Hadn't the man and the car both been standing there for some time? There was less than a two-yard gap between the taxi that pulled away and the next taxi, but Calder plunged through, across the taxi lane, across the traffic and island, coming to a stop directly in front of Imogen's car.

She slammed on her brakes. Calder stepped aside the way a toreador might twist to allow the bull's horns to pass under his chest. He threw open the passenger door.

"Jesus, Duncan!"

"Drive!" he yelled.

"What?"

"Drive. Now. GO!"

Imogen stepped on the accelerator, setting Duncan back in his seat. As she threaded her way neatly through some narrow openings in the traffic, horns blared behind them.

Calder turned around in his seat and peered through the back window. No car from anywhere near where he had been standing was following them. He looked for any other cars waiting along the roadside that could have been alerted, but there was no one.

He settled into his seat. "Sorry about that," he said.

"What the hell were you doing?"

"I'm sorry. I have something very important to tell you. I'm glad we have—"

"—What the hell were you doing?!"

"I'm being followed. They've tried to kill me once already, and I thought—"

"I'm going to pull over. We can discuss."

"Just keep going, please. It's great to see you. We've got half an hour, maybe forty-five minutes until we get to Washington?"

Imogen nodded.

"I sound nuts—" Calder began.

Imogen nodded.

"But there's a plot to subvert the presidential election."

"Does it have to do with Illinois?" asked Imogen, thinking of her own work, of the work she would already be doing if she had not agreed to pick up Duncan.

"No.   It has to do with the Electors themselves."

"Really?" said Imogen, still a bit in shock. But she was also wondering if she wanted to know first about how someone had tried to kill him, or if she wanted some background, a frame of reference.

"I'll begin at the beginning," said Calder. "But first understand that I've come to you because you are the only person I know that I trust to stop this thing. One, you will understand what I'm talking about, and two, you'll have a better idea than I do how to proceed."

"I'm listening," she said.

"I was working closely with a graduate student, Matthew Yamashita, who was doing a demographic survey of Electors for his dissertation using students from my Intro to American Politics class as his polling organization.

"Okay," said Imogen.

"During the protocol coding, he noticed that far too many of the Electors had died suddenly. Seven of them had been replaced because they had died in some kind of accident. Statistically, it's way out of line. Two dying might happen randomly; three, possibly, but seven—and all in accidents—is impossible."

"Okay, but why is he the only person to have noticed this if it is so significant?"

"He was the only one who had data on all of the Electors. There's no national tracking. The whole thing is entirely administered by the parties within each state."

"Right. They've very jealous of their powers. I know," she said, thinking of the mess in Illinois.

"And," he continued, "the only reason Matthew noticed anything was because of the discrepancy between the names he received when the Electors were chosen in late September or early October, which comprised his initial database, and the new Electors."

Imogen looked quizzically at him, taking her eyes momentarily off the road.

"He started calling every Democratic and Republican Elector in America. The list he used had been supplied by the each state's party; and each state had given him their lists in September or October. He started making his survey calls in early December. Seven of the people he tried to contact— seven out of one thousand seventy-six—had died between October and December. All seven died and were replaced in approximately a six-week period.

Imogen said nothing. She found herself glancing into the rearview mirror in case someone were following.

Calder had been worried that when he finally began talking about what he knew he would sound mad. But this was going well. He knew better than to accept Imogen's silence as agreement, but the wheels inside her keen mind were certainly turning.

He began again. "Matthew found these deaths—seven against an expected one or two. So he had a death rate five to ten times higher than the crude death rate."

Imogen was nodding as she drove, but Duncan could tell she still thinking skeptically. Having long ago discarded his own doubts, he found her rational thoroughness frustrating, though that skepticism was probably something he and his colleagues had helped imbue. He was impatient to have her convinced and working with him, but he forced himself to go slowly, to go into detail. He didn't want to betray his impatience.

"I wasn't swayed by that statistic myself," Calder offered. "There was no data about the dead Electors other than what could be gleaned from first and last name and party affiliation. But then Matthew created a demographic profile of the living respondents and ran his mortality rates against those based on census figures for roughly the same demographic group.

"For the period and group he studied, the annual rate was twenty-one per *hundred* thousand, point-two-one for one thousand. We have seven for roughly one thousand, and that for a two-month period--not twelve months. So if we divide—"

"I get the point," said Imogen. She was silent for a moment, staring straight ahead at the road. "That sounds as though it could be significant," she allowed.

"There's more. At first, I knew of only the crude death statistics, and then Matthew died in a hit and run accident in the Arboretum."

"What?! Duncan, I'm so sorry. Are the local police investigating?"

"Yes. But they are not regarding it as a murder."

"And you are, Duncan?"

"I was shocked. Grief-stricken. He was really, really good. Smart. Ambitious. I felt a little as though my own son had been killed. I honestly hadn't been that excited about a student . . . well, since you left . . . I went to his house with his father to get the protocols he'd been working on. But both the protocols and his laptop were gone.

"At the time, I was just upset about the senseless death of someone I felt would really make a contribution and then I can't find the protocols; and the police can't find his laptop. And then one night, someone breaks into my office. Whoever it was, went through all of the Excel files about my work on parties."

"How could you tell that?"

"You click on 'Open Recent,' and it gives you the last four files opened. None of them was anything I had worked on in months. Then, I realize that they'd gotten into my email remotely and looked through my stuff there. At this point, I'm worried, but I haven't made any connection."

Imogen was silent. She wanted to look at the numbers herself. She would reserve judgment until then.

Calder continued: "It turns out that Matthew had sent me his information, but I had deleted the message without reading it. That probably bought me some time. I was able to retrieve the data and I began going through it."

"Okay: so you have some dead Electors. How does all this add up to a plot to overturn the election?"

"Right. I started running through everything Matthew had done. Only Democratic Electors have died, and zero Republicans have died. What's more, the Democratic deaths occurred only in states where there was a Democratic plurality. And, I meant to double-check this, I also think that none of the deaths occurred in states which have regulations against Faithless Electors."

"Who have you told about this?" asked Imogen.

"Just you. "

"Why didn't you go to the police, the F.B.I.?"

"Believe me, I thought about it, but Matthew had clearly told someone other than me, and Matthew is now dead. I called a reporter at the Post, Jerry Ingram. Remember him? He's dead, too. He died within twenty-four hours of Matthew. This thing is operating on a national level. We're talking about people who can kill anyone they want, anywhere they want. They can tap phones and capture email passwords. Only the government, or some organization linked to the government, can do such things."

"So there's a huge conspiracy? Come on."

"I know, but think about it. Who else can operate like this? There must be some complicity on the part of people within various government agencies."

"There are rotten apples in any bunch, Duncan," said

Imogen, irritated that he seemed to be implying that The Bureau was in on anything like this.

"Indeed. Which is why I think it likely some people within the government—if not at the direction of government leaders—are involved in the plot."

"And what is that plot, Duncan? What do you think is going to happen?" asked Imogen, her eyes on the road.

"Whoever they are, they have killed seven Electors and substituted seven plants, who will then change their vote when the time comes."

Imogen nodded, eyes on the road, her face blank. Suddenly a thought occurred to her and she cocked her head: "Wait a minute. How much did Christopher lose by?" she asked.

"By four Electoral College votes . . . or so it seems, since the Electors haven't met to cast their votes yet."

"That's what I thought. Which means only three have to switch their votes, Duncan."

"That bothers me, too. But maybe they figure they can't trust their plants. Maybe they want a margin for error?" Calder paused. "And most important, most significant: even if I'm wrong about the detail, I'm clearly on to something that someone doesn't want known.

"They broke into my office. When I finally retrieved Matthew's data, I saved it in three places. I printed it out and photocopied it twice. Then I made three copies of the information on three different thumb-drives. The first copy and printout, I put in an envelope taped to the underside of my desk. When I checked yesterday, the envelope was gone. The second copy of the printout and the second drive, I mailed to myself. Ten minutes after I got off the phone with you yesterday, my building manager called to tell me that he hadn't known whether or not to let my son into my mailbox."

"You don't have a son," said Imogen.

"I know, but the guy had a driver's license with my

surname and claimed to be my son. The third copy has been in my pocket this whole time." He tapped his breast pocket. "I wanted you to get it in case anything happened to me. And it had to be here quickly, because if this goes through any later investigation is certain to be suppressed."

"When did you become such a conspiracy theorist, Duncan?"

"The closest election in a generation has been overturned once already."

Imogen was no longer listening. At the word "overturned" she began thinking about Illinois again. She would definitely have to finish her work on that today, she thought and then move on to Duncan's data. She could waste no time. It certainly sounded as though Duncan was on to something, but she had to look for herself: there had to be an alternate reading of the data, something Calder had not thought of. Though it made sense as Duncan told it, it was too much to believe.

She would focus on Illinois today, she decided, and then look at Duncan's findings. If there had been tampering and the Democrats had fixed the election there, Illinois' 20 Electoral votes would be going to Christopher instead of Redmond, making Christopher the winner. Calder's conspiracy would have been pointless, even if it were true.

Not realizing that Imogen's mind was racing ahead, Duncan continued. "I think seven Faithless Electors isn't a margin for error. They want a definitive win. Something that cannot be questioned. The higher the number, the more it looks like a vote of conscience, the more it appears to be the will of the people."

"I'm going to take you to my apartment," said Imogen. "Stay there until I get back. You'll be safe there. I have a lot to do today which may work in tandem with your theory. I've been assigned to discover whether there was a pattern that would indicate tampering in the Illinois election. If there was, then the election should go to Christopher anyway—"

"But—"

"So if I uncover tampering, ."

Calder felt blank, flat, exhausted. This was not how he had wanted this conversation to go. He had put up with the fatigue and terror of the past days by looking forward to this moment, as a relay runner might put out of his mind the weakening of his legs and the searing of his lungs by concentrating on the exchange when he could hand off the baton and collapse. Calder had handed off the baton only to see his relay partner hesitate.

Imogen took Calder's sudden silence for the profound disappointment it was.

"I think it's a mistake to go to your apartment," he said. "I have tried very hard not to get anyone else killed. But we can't know what they know. If they got your license plate, or have been tracking me some other way, they will know where you live very soon. They will find us."

Imogen tried to interject.

"They're very thorough, Gen."

"You said they tried to kill you," she said. "How?"

"On my way to the airport. They followed my taxi, drove into us and tried to shove us into oncoming traffic on the First Ave South bridge."

"My God."

"Then they tailed me at the airport," said Calder.

"On the bridge," Imogen began, "you're sure?"

"I'm sure. There's aggressive driving, there's asshole driving, and there's I'm-gonna-kill-you driving. They took a big chance, shoving us across the lanes. Anything could have happened. Luckily, I think the cabby is related to Mario Andretti, and we got out of it."

"Still . . ."

"We only got away from the other car by dropping into oncoming traffic. I have never been so scared in my life."

Imogen was silent, trying to take in all that he had said.

"In fact, I've been frightened for days now. I can't go anywhere without feeling as though I'm being watched."

The car was rolling slowly through rush hour traffic, which now came to a stop. "You are my only hope, and I hate to bring you into all this. But I can't think of anyone else to trust, no one who—" He stopped abruptly. He was very tired, and in the moment before he stopped talking he had been sure he would break down, would begin crying and blubbering.

"Anyway," he began when he felt the storm of emotion had passed. "Until we get some kind of handle on this thing, I think we should stay away from your place. It might be safe, but the consequences of being wrong are too great. Please believe me."

"I do, Duncan." Imogen's skepticism, her methodical habit of mind had been turned upside down. She could see that Duncan's had too, and she did not like the result. He seemed smaller to her, less in control. He had as much as admitted he was fearful of almost everything, but even so, somehow he did not seem to cower. There was a resigned strength in him, she felt. He was by no means beaten yet.

"There's the Marriott Hotel, three and a half blocks from my building. I think you should stay there."

"Fine," said Calder. "If you have to call me, call once, let it ring twice, hang up and then call back. That way I'll know it's you. Otherwise, I'll ignore it."

"I won't call till late afternoon. You look like you need some sleep. We'll get together tonight. I can probably work out whether there's anything more to the tampering claims in Illinois by the end of today. I'll bring my laptop to the hotel tonight, and we'll go over all this all step-by-step. Okay?"

Calder nodded wearily.

"We'll put the hotel on my credit card."

"Why?"

"If it's as you say, they might be attempting to trace you through card receipts. That's what we do in the Department; and I don't see why if they have the resources that they wouldn't do the same."

"I see. Okay. Thank you."

They drew up to the hotel and left the car in the traffic circle while Imogen came in with Calder to pay for the room. "Get a shower, have some food sent up and get some rest." She started to hug him and then thought better of it. "We'll regroup about five or five-thirty. I'll call just before I come over."

Calder smiled, but his face had no light, his eyes no joy.

At The Bureau, Imogen bought herself a large coffee and scooted up to her desk. She set to work on the computer files that had been sent to her from the Illinois Secretary of State's office. As she did so, she glanced at the clock. It was still only 8:15. She stared at the piles of paper on her desk, stared at the computer.

She felt she had already done a full day's work, after the strain of the morning so far. The work on the ballot-tampering would take all day, and would probably mean lunch at her desk; seeing Calder later would not be a relaxing dinner after all. It would be a third full day's worth of work in 24 hours.

For the first hour or so, her thoughts kept being interrupted by Calder's theory. As she would lean back in her chair to wait while the computer scrolled through some operation or ran a calculation, the image of Calder would swim up through her thoughts. His haggard face—the wan smile that was not a smile—tugged at her, distracted her. But by the second hour, anything but the calculations was gone from her mind. She was lost in her work, behind the closed door, her phone on "call forward."

Anyone who had seen her might have been as surprised

to see the pleasure on her face as she had been by the pleasure on Calder's on the night he told her never to let on that work might be fun. It would have been easy to catch her unaware as she worked, for she looked at nothing but the screen. From time to time her hands would emit a few precise, staccato commands and then all would fall silent while she scrolled through pages of figures.

At about 2:30pm, she noticed her coffee had become cold. She looked at the clock on her desk and realized she hadn't yet stopped for lunch. Until that moment, she had not felt hungry, but now hunger came crashing in on her. She had not had breakfast because she had left so early in order to pick up Calder, and now she had worked through lunch.

In the cafeteria, she loaded her tray with popcorn, macaroni salad, two hot dogs, a large soda. Waiting to pay, her hunger increased. Her hands began to tremble slightly, to feel weak. She grabbed a chicken salad sandwich as well.

She forced herself to stay in the cafeteria, knowing she would forget to eat if she were to take the tray back to her desk. She sat by herself and ate everything except the popcorn. She ate heartily, ravenously. When she was done, she sat back from the table as a lioness might finally stand away from her fresh kill. She breathed in slowly, deliberately, willing the food into her system.

As she walked slowly back to her office, munching the popcorn, she thought of Calder for the first time in hours, wondering how he was doing. It was a fleeting thought, though, and by the time she was back at her desk, she was completely focused again. Her face beamed. By four o'clock she was in the home stretch, her concentration interrupted only occasionally by rumblings of revolt from her stomach.

Calder had taken Imogen's advice. He had ordered breakfast to his room, eaten laconically, showered and collapsed into bed. Perhaps it was the dampness of his hair or some deep-seated adjustment to the trauma, but whatever the reason, he dreamed again of Matthew, dead in the Arboretum. In his mind he felt how cold it was to die. He could smell the heady, dank decay of leaves and ferns around the body, its fullness not merely an odor but a resonance in the sinuses.

He saw clearly the gritty muck covering the leaves which partially hid Matthew's body, felt a chill of death and a sudden rush of warmth. And then it was not Matthew, but himself, dead by the side of the road. Only he was not dead. He felt himself struggling for air, as though a pillow had been placed over his face. Calder's mouth was stuffed with those same gritty rotting leaves. A crowd stood around, looking at him. Imogen was there.

A thick-set man in a blue blazer was corralling the gapers, telling them Calder was dead; there was nothing more to see. Calder tried to raise his hand to point at another man, to accuse him of causing his death, but his hand would not rise. He tried to speak, but his mouth was stopped up with decay. He saw Imogen walking away, saddened, and he ached to hold her, ached to be held by her, cradled by her.

"I'll be goddamned," said Imogen, smiling at her screen. "This is too perfect."

Having found a pattern of late returns in Democratic-controlled districts, she had turned her attention to the Republican-controlled districts. Something a historian friend once said resounded in her mind—"Your job isn't done when you find what you want to find: if you find a box buried away that no one else has seen, and it contains a letter or a document supporting your theory, you still have to regard and consider everything else in the box, even if—particularly if—that investigation ends up killing your theory." Her second run-through included testing the times that Republican-controlled precincts had reported and what they reported. Imogen clicked "print."

She pushed her chair slightly back and dialed Pollack's extension. "It's Gen. I've got it. Yes, done. Yes. It's printing now," she said. "Well . . . let me just show you when I get there. Yes. I ran it two different ways and came up with exactly the same result. I'll be over as soon as it's done printing." She walked around to the front of her desk and stretched; then to the printer, where she checked the page number of the sheet rolling out into the tray. She walked back to her desk and slipped on her shoes. She stood up and re-tucked her shirt into her skirt. Grabbing the final page from the printer, she set off for the Assistant Director's office.   It was 4:35 p.m.

When she arrived, Doug Pollack and Tom Kurtz were standing next to Pollack's desk. Each wore an identical expression of hopeful eagerness tinged with worry. Imogen put the report on the desk.

"Did they do it? Were they stuffing the box?" he asked without glancing at the report.

"Yes," said Imogen.

"And was the Illinois Secretary covering it up?"

"I doubt it," she rejoined. "It's quite subtle."

"Okay," said Pollack, "it was probably too much to ask for. But the Democrats did it? You're sure?"

"Then we've got 'em," said Kurtz, a bit too elated.

"The Republicans did it," said Imogen, relishing the moment.

Both men now looked at Imogen with suspicion. "What do you mean?" said Pollack. "The Republicans lost."

"As I was going through all the data—I mean I want to be thorough after all—I noticed something."

"What else was there?"

"Well, I also looked at the predominantly Republican precincts. I thought they might function as some kind of control . . . you know."

"Okay," said Pollack. "And?"

"And they were both doing it."

"What?"

"They were both waiting to report the results, but in the late-reporting Republican-leaning precincts, there was a mini-surge in Republican votes. I can see why you weren't getting any cooperation from the Illinois people. Both sides knew they had done it, so neither was going to point the finger at the other and invite scrutiny of their own reporting methods."

"They were both doing it?" said Kurtz, incredulous.

"Yes," said Imogen.

Pollack sat down behind his desk. Kurtz looked profoundly lost. "What the hell do we do with that?" Kurtz asked no one in particular. "I mean, how do we know the true election results?"

"I thought of that, too," said Imogen. Pollack was not looking at her. He was holding his head in his hands and staring flatly at his desk top. "So far," she continued, "it's only right at the end that any engineering was taking place. If anything, the Republicans were stuffing more ballots earlier, which prompted the Democrats, who were ahead, to hold off reporting so they could add votes. But in the end, they didn't need to."

"Why does everything have to be so damned complicated?" Pollack whined.

"It isn't complicated at all," said Imogen. "My report has it all. Tom and his team can begin investigating who was doing what exactly. It's still important that we quash this kind of behavior. But so far as the question of the soundness of the outcome in Illinois, I can say with certainty that the result stands."

Pollack held Imogen's report absently, staring into the middle-distance. Kurtz seemed deep in his own thoughts. As Imogen turned to go back to her office, she almost felt as though she should apologize. It was ten minutes of five. She had time to go home and change before she met Calder at the hotel.

CHAPTER ELEVEN

As she reached her car, keys in hand, Imogen stood a moment, wondering whether it was just ordinary dislike of parking garages that accounted for the chill across her shoulders, or whether Duncan's warning about going home was part of it too. She was tense. The muscles between her shoulder blades felt taut and knotted, as though she had exercised too strenuously and then caught her breath by resting with her back against something terrifically cold.

The freezing tightness radiated from her back and seemed to clutch at her heart. Her unease was exacerbated by having come through the tunnel from the Bureau, which was used primarily by witnesses and informants who didn't want to be seen going in and out of the building. It was long and subterranean, with several blind turns. The uniformed guards sitting at either end of the corridor did little to reduce its spookiness.

The public parking-garage adjacent to the Bureau was similar to many another underground parking facility. Functional, inhospitable. It was like being below decks on a sinking ship or underwater in the belly of a whale. The sound of cars traveling across the metal dividers between slabs of concrete rumbled with the familiar shock and groan of buckling metal. The low ceilings and very poor lighting set the nerves on edge, filling every encounter with another human being with distrust and foreboding. The concrete was exposed and pipes jutted out, lean ribs on a very hungry beast. Echoes sounded everywhere, their source indeterminable, masked by exhaust fans rumbling like unrelenting indigestion.

Imogen's heart beat harder within the cold grasp that held her. She opened the car and sat down inside, where she paused again. Maybe she shouldn't go home, she thought. What if Duncan was right?

"Damn," she hissed as she started the car. Her breath suddenly came more easily, and she began talking to herself. "Okay," she began, reviewing everything aloud, "I haven't even seen Duncan's evidence yet. He is a highly esteemed scholar—no one knows that better than I do—but this is too much. It can't be." This soliloquy calmed her, but she turned left out of the parking garage in the direction of Duncan's hotel.

Though she sometimes worried about the number of conversations she had with herself, Imogen found that speaking her thoughts was often a great help. Just as proofreading something one has written by reading it aloud is more effective than merely scanning it for errors, speaking thoughts aloud meant putting them into words, which could then be examined. Her faith in this method was strong, but as strong as it was, it didn't entirely quell the nagging belief that she was going mad, and that her talking to herself was not so much a way of making sense of the world as a sign of loneliness and boredom. Would she end up with a cat as her only companion?

"Still," she said, as though making ready to contradict a sensitive acquaintance, "Duncan's not crazy. He's not hearing voices. There is a hunted look about him, it's true; but it feels real. Lord knows, he's not given to wild theories. But maybe this is grief bottled up and now spilling over, infecting and souring his intellect." Imogen considered this as she changed lanes. "But he must have known I would need to see the data before getting on board."

Though Duncan was now out of bed and dressed, his thoughts were blunted, vacillating within an umbral nether state of confusion, grogginess and fear. He had not slept well. He moved restlessly about the hotel room, unable to focus on any one thing for more than an instant, unable even to concentrate long enough for the television to be distracting. Though it clamored for attention, the television remained merely background noise. Calder would find himself sitting on the edge of his bed, staring toward it but not seeing it. The next moment he would be staring out his window at the scaffolding covering the Capitol, with no sense in his mind of what he had just seen. His thoughts were of Imogen, of the time they had wasted.

There was no rancor in his observation. It was merely that, an observation. He was anxious to begin, and he regarded every moment not spent doing something as time wasted, as giving the conspiracy more leverage. He wondered where she was. She had said she would call or come by five-thirty, and it was now past that time. He hoped she was all right.

Calder worried about Imogen; and as he worried, the dark dread he felt at their predicament exploded into white rage as it rose within him, as blood flowing blue within the vein suddenly runs red as it wells up through the wound, tinged by the open air, its change so swift and complete there is little thought to ascertaining where in fact the alteration from one to the other occurred.

True to his Calvinist roots, Calder blamed himself first, his anger not so blind nor thoughtless as to lack recrimination for himself at having brought this danger to her. For danger it was, made all the more dangerous for Imogen because she was not yet convinced of the absolute need for caution in all things. He thought of her as she had been that morning, sunny, beautiful, canny.

Calder had liked seeing her again. The intervening years had been good to her. She looked well and her mind was as sharp as ever. He had been concerned that away from academia she might have settled into a routine which would have dulled her acuity. Calder noted happily that after Imogen's initial shock over his findings, she had jumped right in, questioning, challenging. Now that he had her more or less on his side, he thought, they could move quickly, could get the information out. But to whom, and how?

As Imogen drove through freezing, congested DC streets toward Calder's hotel, she tried calm herself, tried to come up with alternate explanations for what was going on. She would reserve judgment, she told herself, until she had seen what Duncan had to show her. She would want confirmation of his figures, too.

Her briefcase and laptop computer were nestled in the back seat of her car. "He had better be right," she said aloud. "To be this scared over what could be nothing...." She let that thought trail off.

"Nevertheless," she began, "I think I should act as though it were all true—take no chances." Calder had come to her, he had said, as the only person who would both understand the significance of the findings and who could do something about the plot. She had liked being in control; had liked the idea of the reversed roles between Duncan and herself. And despite his somewhat wild manner that morning, she thought, he had looked good. But now, she felt, neither of them was in control. She had to know the full story.

"But first," she said to herself as she turned sharply into a drive-through Cash Machine facility, "they could trace us. We should only spend cash from now on, I think." She withdrew five hundred dollars, as much as she could take out at one time.

Duncan had taken to pacing back and forth along the length of the room. It was now five forty-five, and nothing from Imogen. He was worried and agitated. He wanted to get on with whatever they were going to do. Though he had been frightened over the past days, he had been comforted by a sense of purpose, a feeling that all would be all right if he could only get to Washington D.C. alive. Now, that he was here, he was impatient to embark on the next phase, but not knowing what that next phase might be grated on him.

Nothing more would happen that day, he felt sure. Imogen would want to review his data, and he would have to endure it; but with every passing moment, he felt the next day's work slipping away as well. What if she didn't arrive until after eight? he thought. What if she were so tired when she arrived she could only get through half of it?

As he paced, he would walk to one end of the room by the front door, turn and walk back to the other end, where the television was on. He would stare at it momentarily and then look out the window. A moment later he would walk back toward the front door. Occasionally he would stop at the door and peer out through the security spy-hole with its fisheye lens.

Grief at Matthew's death had turned to anger in Duncan. It festered, it nagged; it smoldered dully for as long as a day at times and then burst upon him as a raging madness. In his more lucid moments the anger that occasionally flared within him was dismaying and frightening to him; for upon reflection, as he would calm himself, he was sure that within his anger, he wanted nothing more nor less than to kill those responsible for killing Matthew--the country and the president be damned.

Calder knew, too, that anger of the kind he carried about with him smoldering, was itself damnation, a single-mindedness that bred mistakes, that robbed and diverted energy from the true purpose, which was to stop the plot and bring the conspirators to justice; and in those lucid moments, when the fever of rage had broken, he knew that true purpose, knew he must guard against giving in to blind rage;

knew that if Matthew's death were truly to be avenged, it would be by finishing what Matthew had begun. As he paced about the room, he would touch the thumb-drive in his shirt pocket from time to time.

Imogen parked outside the hotel and walked in to the front desk. "I reserved room 348 with my credit card this morning," she said to the desk attendant. "I used the wrong one. Could I just pay for it in cash? Have you sent it through yet?

"Let me just check," said the desk attendant. "No," he said, "it hasn't been posted yet."

Imogen proffered the money for two nights.

"Cash is never a problem," said the clerk, smiling at her. He was jocular and good looking, athletically built. He might as easily have been a bartender in a trendy nightclub, for he seemed ready at a moment's notice to begin some light banter with anyone with whom he came into contact.

Imogen knocked twice at Calder's door. "I wonder," said Imogen as she walked into the room, "Do you think they have any of those little liquor bottles in here?"

Calder squatted in front of the little refrigerator in the alcove outside the bathroom, opened the cupboard above it and pointed. "Wild Turkey?" he asked, remembering that it was her drink.

"Thank you, yes," she said as she let her computer and briefcase fall to the bed. She sat heavily on a corner. She realized there was only one bed in the room. She wondered if this would be a problem.

Calder remained crouched in front of the cupboard above the diminutive refrigerator, deciding what it was he wanted to drink. There were three of the tiny bottles of Wild Turkey in a row, one behind the other. The Scotch was not particularly tempting until Calder found a tiny bottle of Glenlivet behind a miniature Cutty Sark. He pulled the paper wrapping off the tops of two glasses, rinsed them and poured two bottles into Imogen's glass, one into his. He wished it could have been four bottles.

He walked over to Imogen. "There are two in this glass. There's one little bottle left."

Imogen took a long sip. She breathed deeply and took another, though smaller, sip.

"I want to see your data, Duncan. I need to know what's going on. I think I believe you, but…"

"But you need to see it for yourself. You need to convince yourself. I knew you would."

"So, let's get at it," she said and cleared a spot on the bureau across from the bed. Imogen scooted her chair in and began arranging the top of the bureau as though it were her desktop. She handed her empty glass to Calder. "Would you fill this up?" she asked. He took the glass.

When he returned, she thanked him for the drink, and said: "Okay. Data drive, please. And while I'm getting it set up and saved on my hard drive, tell me again your methodology. How you, or what was his name?"

"Matthew. Matthew found it all."

"How Matthew arrived at this conclusion."

Calder began first with the numbers. Seven dead. He pulled out a sheet on which he had earlier written what he remembered the Census Bureau's Vital Statistics numbers had been. "Actually," he said, withdrawing the paper, "I think it would be better for me not to prejudice you any further, but to allow you to come to your own conclusion."

"No," said Imogen. "I need the data. I'm basically going to try to disprove the significance of what you've found; and if I can't, I'll believe what you say is true."

"Good," said Calder. "Fine .... as it should be."

After only 15 minutes, Imogen sat back. "Somebody's killing Electors," she said. "Listen. Is your phone off?."

Calder looked at it. "It's still in airplane mode."

"Good. Turn it off completely. The next opportunity, you should go to a cash machine and withdraw as much money as you can—somewhere not near here. We are going to have to be very careful. Is there any other kind of bourbon?" she asked.

Calder poured each of them another drink.

She took the glass from his hand, their fingers touching briefly. His hand lingered a moment in the air and then withdrew.

Imogen took a deep drink of the bourbon and pushed back from the bureau. "There is no way this is random. Combined with the attempt on your life, Matthew's death, Ingram's death," she continued, "I have no reason to believe this is not a plot."

Calder smiled slightly. Though she did not work at a university, he thought, she was an academic at heart. No one could pile on the negatives as she just had without having at least one foot firmly within the academy.

"And," she said, wondering what the hell Duncan was smiling about, "though I remain skeptical regarding the involvement of the F.B.I. or some other governmental agency, I also agree that we need to be very careful, which is why we have to turn off cell phones, only use cash."

"So what do we do now?" asked Calder.

"I'm not entirely sure, but the absolute first thing we must do is eat. I'm starving. I refuse to think anymore until I get some food in me."

"If you think we're safe here, we could eat in the restaurant downstairs," he offered.

"Yes," she said, knowing she would have said yes to anywhere at that point.

Dinner was not the jocular, old-friends-together event Imogen had hoped for when she had first spoken with Duncan. She marveled that it had only been yesterday

---

afternoon when they had spoken. She had done so much, so much had happened, and so much was now different that her impression was of a much longer time. Theirs was a quiet table. Both were famished, both were lost in their respective worlds. The bread they were served upon being seated was gone immediately, as was the second round of bread.

The waiter made an elaborate display of getting his hands out of the way when he served the soup. "Hungry, it would seem," he said smiling. Calder and Imogen said nothing as they began to eat. He dropped off some more bread, too.

The restaurant was somber but comfortable, its low light and deep colors in sharp contrast to most suburban hotel restaurants. Calder pushed back from the table slightly and examined his surroundings, not as he had over the past few days, with defense or escape in mind, but with pleasure. The chairs were of a dark wood, upholstered in thick, dark green fabric. A candle to one side of the table was the principle light source. The tablecloths were a flat, parchment color. He had eaten only airplane food or cafeteria food for some time, it seemed, and he was enjoying this respite. It was comfortable, snug, safe.

"Not quite Place Pigalle," said Genny, referring to Calder's favorite restaurant in Seattle. "But it'll do, I think."

"I almost feel I could let my guard down a bit .... Almost."

"I know," she said, and they both fell silent for a time.

"What are we going to do?" asked Calder finally.

"I've been thinking about that a bit. I've considered letting my boss, Douglas Pollack, in on it, but I have reservations about that. I trust him. There is no way he is in on any of this. None. But he would go at this through proper channels, and we cannot be sure of anyone else."

"Yes," said Calder. "Whatever we do, it will have to be surprising."

"What we need to do," she continued, "is something of an end run. We need somehow to get the information to someone we can trust who is above Pollack's level, so that when we tell Pollack and he goes about it through channels, the facts are known somewhere else, too. If we did it like that, it would go a long way toward stopping the conspiracy and toward exposing the conspirators themselves."

"That's good," said Calder. "Who are you thinking of?"

"That's it, I'm afraid. That's as far as I've gotten. Was Ingram the only reporter you thought to call?"

"He's the only one I knew who would take me seriously," said Calder

"I think you underestimate yourself—a professor of Political Science, a specialist in Elections and the Electoral College says he has evidence that the election is going to be rigged?"

"In any case, when I found out Ingram was dead, I got really worried that I might die myself at any moment. I tried to email you the data, but they'd changed my password. But it's good thinking. Do you know anyone?" asked Calder.

"Not really. Not to know and trust. And frankly, I'm not sure what would happen next. I'm not permitted to talk to the press, actually. All of my directions and communications come through Pollack. All my reports go to him, or someone he designates. If this thing is some big conspiracy or cover-up, I'd be the first one to be discredited and sacrificed, which wouldn't help our cause, and having broken protocol so brazenly, there's no way I could count on Pollack's help.

"It's all quite paramilitary when you get right down to it. Chain of command, and all that. I suppose it has to be that way for one reason and another, but it's sickening what it can do to people. You overhear people or have conversations where people speak with this spooky reverence, this perverse relish for their higher-ups *as* their higher ups."

Calder raised a finger to interject--

"It may be," Imogen continued, "that the chain of command is necessary. We don't know whether it's necessary because we've never tried a different way, and I find my skin crawling at the way so many people so unthinkingly leap to the idea that they have betters who know what's best for them; that there are things they should not know and cannot do, which are best left to higher-ups."

"Is your boss, Pollack, like that?"

"Well, as one of the higher-ups he has a degree of autonomy ... I mean, he's not one of these craven toadies I've been talking about."

"But?" said Calder sensing she was talking around the point.

"But, yeah. He is somewhat."

"Then I think you're right, and he should be the second person we tell," said Calder.

"Which puts us back where we were," sighed Imogen.

"It does."

Their food arrived, along with the wine Calder had ordered, and they began eating, this time slowly, savoring the flavors instead of attacking as they had before.

Their meal and their surroundings fed and rejuvenated them far deeper than mere sustenance. Calder and Imogen relaxed.

Their heads became clearer despite the wine. Calder felt he had finally gained the distance he needed to see their predicament in perspective. It had taken sleep, time and food; and above all, it had taken Imogen, her expertise, her good sense, her faith. The warmth and gratitude he felt for her at that moment seemed boundless.

"I have it," she said putting down her fork.

"Okay..." said Calder.

"How do we know we can trust someone?"

Calder shrugged.

"By knowing they can gain nothing by this plot being

carried out," she said. "Who in fact has the most to lose if this plot is carried out?"

"The president-elect?" said Calder.

Imogen shook her head. "We couldn't get to see her without going through the channels we're trying so hard to avoid."

"Then ... ?"

"Her campaign manager, Jim Novaczech. I worked with him once a few years back—did some checking into some things he thought were fishy. I was loaned to him from the FBI's Corruption Unit. We had a good working relationship."

Calder's heart leapt. "So he knows your work. He'd believe you."

"But I think you should go," said Imogen. "I need to be prepared to take this to Pollack. It'll sound much better to him coming from me, whereas with my recommendation to Novaczeck, he'll listen to you. You're my mentor after all."

Calder nodded. "Okay."

"I have his number in my phone up in the room. We'll call him. Try to set up an appointment."

"The sooner the better," said Calder.

Imogen looked at her watch. "It's nine-thirty," she said. "We can call and leave a message, but another half-hour one way or the other isn't going to matter, since he probably isn't going to get the message until the morning. Right? I'm enjoying this," she said, making a sweeping gesture. "I need this after the day we've had. I don't know how you stood it for as long as you did. I'd have cracked long ago."

"Don't be so sure I haven't," he said. He looked around the room, too impatient to want to sit a moment longer. He was, however, growing accustomed to taking his cues from Imogen, and he did as she recommended. "I feel so powerless sometimes. My dreams are horrifying. You can't know...."

Calder was glad she could not know, was resolute in his

desire that she would not know. For the violence and anger he felt frightened him and would have at the least disturbed her.

"We'll go call, Duncan," said Imogen.

"I'm sorry. I was thinking about something else."

"But you want to go?"

"No, it's okay. You're right. Let's sit and talk."

Calder paid the bill and they lingered over their drinks for another hour or so, talking about her life, her work. Calder found himself prompting her more than he might have otherwise because he did not want to talk about his own work, nor his frustrations, his lack of confidence, his feeling of irrelevance. Most of all, he did not want to think, let alone speak of the crushing blow Matthew's death had been.

For her part, Imogen had at first been pleased to talk at length about herself to someone for whom she had an abiding respect and warmth. It had been gratifying. Each episode or anecdote she related, she found, grew or diminished in her own esteem by his reaction to it. Finally, however, Imogen realized he was not so much interested in her as loathe to discuss himself. It was not modesty on his part, nor a seemly reticence to toot his own horn. It was mendacity, a brave face maintained by a subtle program of omission.

Imogen guessed at Calder's feelings, his depression regarding his own work and the way things had turned out so far. She knew he was fueled by new students, new challenges matted within a frame of mutual respect, much of which, she guessed, was no longer forthcoming. The profound sadness and pointlessness he was unable to hide from her, as he had been unable mask his disappointment at the breakup of his marriage, touched her more deeply than if he had spoken of it. She knew he had it within him to rally, to rebound from the abyss of meaninglessness, but she wondered about his will to do so. She worried that the tight control he kept over himself was exhausting him, eroding that inner strength which was among his principle attractions.

Finally, they went upstairs. Duncan sat at the foot of the bed, staring at the wall as Imogen left to call Novaczeck's from the payphone in the lobby.

Imogen found a phone and dialed the number.

"Jim," she said when voice mail picked up. "It's Imogen Trager. We worked together a few years ago when I was loaned to you from the Public Corruption Unit. I'm calling because I have information the president-elect needs. I am concerned about leaks within the Justice Department, so I am not going at this the normal way. What I have found could possibly implicate many levels of government, and I need to get the information to someone I know and trust; and who is in a position to do something. This has to be dealt with before Monday. Please call my office phone, my cell doesn't seem to be working properly. I need you to speak with a friend of mine, Professor Duncan Calder, who brought me this information. It will be him you will talk to, not me. He has some startling data you need to see." She gave the number, repeated it and hung up.

Across town, Jim Novaczeck returned to his office from the bathroom, shuffled over to his desk and collapsed into his chair. He rubbed his face and eyes. He noticed he had a voicemail message. "Probably Anne," he said to himself, now annoyed that his wife had called and he had not picked up. He dialed his pass-code. "Tell the truth," he told himself. "You were in the bathroom. For God's sake, it is the truth.... but will she believe it?"

The message was from Imogen Trager. He had heard she was one of the investigators into the Illinois mess. His thoughts ran quickly—maybe there was something damaging about the Illinois result after all. He would need to hear this, whatever it was, the sooner the better, and if it was as important as Imogen felt it was, he would need to hear it first hand, not delegate the meeting. He flipped through his phone's contact list and saw her home number listed, along with her cell and work number. Maybe he could catch her at home.

Across the Potomac in Arlington, the phone rang.

The message machine picked up and gave Imogen's standard greeting, her voice small in the almost empty room. The message machine flashed its red light in the darkness. The only light in the room came from outside on the street where the street lamps threw long, cool diffuse light across the far walls through the sheer curtains, the pleats and folds in the curtains throwing slender, web-like shadows across the floor and walls. The machine beeped. Nearby, in a parked Buick, a tiny electronic beep sounded, and another recording began.

"Yeah. Hi, Imogen. It's Jim Novaczeck. I hoped I might catch you at home so I could hear a little more about all this. I'll call your office, too, but in case you hear this first, you can call me right now. Is this about the Illinois result? I'm putting Professor Calder's name on the list with the security guard. I've got a full day tomorrow. Can't move anything. Have Professor Calder come by the office at seven tomorrow evening. Same office as before."

CHAPTER TWELVE

December 16, 2016

Imogen and Duncan stared at one another across the bed.

"Which side do you want?" she said, as casually as she could.

"I can take that chair," said Calder. "Really."

Imogen thought a moment, then said, "No. Pick a side. We both need a good sleep, and we need to be sharp."

"Doesn't matter," said Calder, looking away. He rubbed his eyes and massaged his scalp.

"Then I'll take this side," she said, indicating the side she was already on.

"Those are your only clothes, aren't they?" said Calder looking up at her.

Imogen nodded.

"I've got a T-shirt you can have. It should be pretty long on you. I'll get it. You can have the bathroom first."

"You go first," she said. "I could do with a bath."

He retrieved a clean T-shirt and handed it to her.

In the bathroom, he felt disoriented. Sleeping during the day had helped but confused his internal clock still further after the flight. He had to remind himself constantly that he'd arrived in Washington only that morning.

He tried to think about the next day, and what it would hold. He tried to think of anything other than Imogen sliding into the bathtub. He could almost see her. As he brushed his teeth, it seemed the most natural thing that she should be bathing and talking to him, her long red hair floating in the currents, her breasts rising out of the water like miniature islands.

But she was not there, he was taking too long, and she was probably growing impatient.

And what the hell was he doing thinking such things when there were people out there trying to kill them both? If he had met Genny again at a convention, or had had some research to do in Washington, it might have been different.

"All yours," he said as he came out of the bathroom.

Imogen had taken off her shoes and stockings. She had hung the stockings across the bottom of the hanger on which she had hung her jacket. Her blouse was open at the neck. As he looked at her, he had the sensation that her body was in conflict with her clothes, scarcely contained by them and chafing to get out. He practically blushed at the thought, remembering his vision of her in the tub.

As they passed in the narrow alcove outside the bathroom, they turned sideways to face one another. Duncan, now barefoot, wearing only a T-shirt and slacks, felt an unmistakable heat brush across his chest as they passed, and he averted his eyes.

Imogen closed the door softly behind her and let out a heavy sigh. As they had passed she had looked at the T-shirt held taut by his broad shoulders, and had glanced at his powerful arms. It was a chest to press against, she thought. She wanted to melt into its firmness, to feel the strength of those arms locked gently around her waist. In some memory that only the body itself holds, she actually felt the pressure of hands across the small of her back, replayed as vividly as though it were happening right then, the humming, tingling sensation of softness yielding to firmness, the boundaries between selves blurring.

The hot bath was a poor substitute for that heat she craved, she thought as she reclined in the tub, but it would do the trick. Before she began washing, she lay back, eyes closed, and sank beneath the surface, immersing her face. Her mother's words floated to her under the water from out of the liquid silence: "There's nothing so bad in this world a hot bath can't cure." Imogen smiled at the thought as she rose out of the water, her chin up, letting the weight of the water pull her hair straight behind her.

"If you only knew," she whispered to her mother. She longed for human contact such as she dared dream was possible with Duncan. The bath, she realized, would cure none of these ills. It would only forestall feeling, acting as a weak surrogate. Imogen chided herself for thinking beyond the next few days, but as she soaked in the tub her mind kept casting itself forward.

She toweled off and pulled her hair back in a pony tail. She pulled on her panties and Duncan's T-shirt. She had hoped momentarily it would have some scent of him but it was freshly laundered. When she stepped quietly out of the bathroom, she found the bedroom dark. Duncan was asleep. His breathing was shallow and calm.

As her eyes adjusted, she made out his form. She smiled. He had taken quite literally the "my side, your side" idea, for he lay on his side, seeming to cling to the very edge of the bed, one leg swung out from underneath the covers. He was occupying not more than eighteen inches of the queen-size bed. Imogen settled herself under the covers and folded her hands across her chest. She looked over at Calder and sighed quietly, wishing she could sleep as easily.

An hour later, as sleep slowly crept through her, Calder began to stir. His recurrent dream was upon him: he saw Matthew's body and then he was Matthew—dead, but not dead, his cries for help stopped by dead leaves, as Satan's minions had had their mouths stopped up with ashes. He moaned unintelligibly, grasped at the air. His body twisted and his hands flexed and unflexed into fists. "No!" he yelled. "I'm alive . . . don't leave . . . got to tell"

"Duncan," she said turning to him and clasping his shoulder.

With a swiftness she would not have dreamed possible his left hand swung out in a wide arc and he dealt her a blow on the shoulder that made her fingers tingle.

"Duncan, wake up."

His arms flailed wildly and she retreated further.

"Duncan, wake up. It's Imogen . . . Duncan?"

"Imogen," he called. "Gen—" His arms stopped flailing and his breathing became more regular.

"I'm here, Duncan. I'm here."

Calder's arms opened toward her. Tentatively, she took his hands in hers, her hands closing across the backs of his hands. She shook them gently. He drew her toward him, his eyes still closed. "I knew," he said. "I knew."

Imogen shunted closer to him. She stroked his hair then drew his head to her chest. Duncan sighed. Still holding his head with one arm, Imogen settled under the sheets. When she had made herself comfortable, she drew him in closer.

He was bathed in sweat, and his heart knocked wildly against her stomach. She continued stroking his hair. Duncan nuzzled his cheek just above her left breast.

Slowly, the storm faded within him. She no longer felt his heart. His breathing came regularly, slow and even. His warmth spread across her. She twisted slightly, throwing one of her legs over his, but it was another hour before she finally fell asleep

Duncan woke first, confused, his head on Imogen's chest, their bodies entangled. He had a vague memory of his nightmare, and if it was true he had acted out in his sleep, he guessed that his need, his weakness, was the reason they had slept so closely. Generally he kept himself and his emotions on a very short leash, and he felt ashamed at the prospect of such a display; moreover, he felt betrayed by his subconscious. Flashes and images hinted at more, but he chose not to try remembering now. Best to keep the door closed on what he felt for Imogen—to keep his passion for her at bay.

Breakfast began in an awkward silence, neither wishing to mention what had happened in the night. Finally, Imogen began laying a plan for the day. "In a couple of minutes, I'll go see if Novaczeck called. I think we should write out as succinctly as possible what we believe is happening. After you've seen Novaczeck, we will want to include Pollack. I think we need a report detailing your methodology, your theory. We need both the printout and your report, which will have all the numbers. Pollack won't look at the actual data, only the summary, which, if you don't mind, I'd like to write. I know how to phrase things in the language he responds to."

Calder, his mouth full of bacon and eggs, merely nodded. His dominant thought that morning was of strategy. He timed his mouthfuls so as to excuse himself from speaking. Just as she finished what she was saying, he would take a mighty forkful, allowing him to ruminate rather than reply. Betrayed by his subconscious once, he didn't want to say anything personal or compromising.

Imogen left the table to check messages and make her phone call.

"You meet Novaczeck tonight," she said as she returned. "I'll drop you at Novaczeck's building, and then I'll go to a little coffee place I like. I'll copy the data onto a drive to give to Pollack."

"Make two copies, plus one for yourself," said Calder.

"Okay," said Imogen warily.

"Because I'm worried. This feels like the homestretch, and in the homestretch people sometimes start thinking too much about the finish and not enough about finishing. They make mistakes. What if Novaczeck doesn't believe me? What if we can't trust Pollack?"

Imogen nodded. "Okay." She did not like the suggestion that Pollack was in any way implicated. Though she made fun of him sometimes and saw his shortcomings all too clearly, he was intelligent, committed and just. He had been very helpful to her, instrumental in her quick rise within the Department. She bristled and tried in vain not to show it.

"You think I'm paranoid, unable to trust anyone. Well, paranoia has served me well thus far. Let's just keep it with us a little farther."

Imogen faced away from Calder toward the laptop screen. She made no move for perhaps as long as a minute. Finally, she turned to him. "Okay," she said. "After you've talked with Novczeck, call me at the coffee place." She wrote down the number. They know me there, and I can wait for your call," she said.

At 6:15, they drove into town in the fading light. To Calder the city looked malevolent, fairly breathing with hostility. "Back in Seattle," he thought, "it will be getting dark soon, too, even though it's three hours behind."

His old life at home might have seemed a kind of slow death, but at least it was safe and comfortable. With each glimpse of the Capitol as they drove, his heart sank further. He was committing, finally, to a course of action; and while he believed in its soundness, he doubted perhaps for the first time in his life his ability to carry out what he had begun.

"Freedom from fear, that's what America promises its people," he thought to himself. "But at what cost? Democracy is predicated on constant vigilance."

He was thinking of Matthew again. He was thinking of revenge. But revenge was not enough. This corruption had to be stopped.

Calder's own passion worried him. As they crested a hill and came again within sight of the Capitol, descending farther into the realm of politics and politicians, who must take things under advisement, must make sure things appear in the best light, must decide not so much what is right and wrong as what can and can't be done, Calder worried that to a presidential aide he would seem a naïve freak with a conspiracy theory.

"You're quiet," said Imogen.

"I'm sorry. I was thinking about Matthew. Doing exactly what I had said we were not to do: think beyond the finish."

Imogen nodded, not wanting to press matters further. She, too, had been thinking beyond the finish.

"We've got to stay sharp," he said aloud, though more for himself than for Imogen's benefit.

She took it as a rebuke to her own unspoken thoughts. Duncan was on break from school, she had been thinking, and she had some vacation time coming.

"I was thinking," she said. "After this is over, whether it be today or tomorrow"—she hesitated, first because she was thinking too far ahead, and second because she was unsure of his response.

"I thought," she began again, "you and I might get away for a little while . . . together . . . after all this."

Duncan turned to her "That would be great," he said, astonished.

"I'm . . . I'm sort of house-sitting for a friend in Philadelphia. He's an anthropologist at Temple. He and his wife are away in Rome for the year. The people who have rented their house won't be moving in until February. They asked me to look in on the place now and again. It's a wonderful city, Philly, and they live very close to the center of town in Queen Village."

"That would be great," he said again.

"They—" she began.

Calder held up his hand. "It sounds wonderful. I'd like to go with you. I'm just—"

"You're right," she said. "You're right. Let's get through today."

They drove the last few blocks in silence.

Imogen pulled the car up in front of Novaczeck's building. "You've got the number," she said. "It's almost over, Duncan."

"Yes," he said distantly as he got out.

Novaczeck's office was on the fifth floor. Calder told the guard he had an appointment. Verifying this on his log-sheet, the guard had him sign in and directed him to the elevators.

The ring of the bell as the elevator reached the fifth floor sounded shrilly in the empty office building. The heavy brass doors seemed at first unwilling to part, and when they finally did it seemed a great effort. Calder walked to his left, as the guard had directed, past the fire exit and across the wide hall toward Novaczeck's office, 513. There seemed to be no one else about, and Calder's footsteps echoed.

It was an old building. The air itself seemed to belong to another age. Calder fancied he smelled cigar smoke. The hallway was wide and polished to a high gloss. The walls were of deeply stained wood, interrupted here and there by sandblasted pebble glass. The only sign of change since the late Thirties or early Forties was the fire exit with its heavy door painted a pale blue and with two Day-Glo signs warning that it was an emergency exit only and that alarms would sound.

The door to 513 was ajar. Seeing it was only the receptionist's area, Duncan knocked lightly and walked in. From here, there were two doors. One, to the left, had the name Cerutti painted on the pebble glass, the other, Novaczeck's.

This door was open too. Calder knocked and walked in. "Mr. Novaczeck?" he called. He could see the top of Novaczeck's head over the back of his swivel chair facing out toward the city. Calder took a tentative step nearer. Blood dripped from Novaczeck's hand. Calder dared not step any closer. He leaned forward, craning his neck to look at Novaczeck, and saw, or imagined he saw, an eruption of flesh just inside Novaczeck's left shoulder, a little below the collarbone.

A flash of clarity split the darkness of Calder's mounting panic. Just as everything had seemed to be happening in slow motion in the taxi on the way to the airport, Calder now, again, had the sensation of hyper-clarity. To his left he thought something moved. He recoiled from the room as two silenced shots erupted from a crack in the door connecting Novaczeck's and Cerutti's offices. Calder winced and twisted as plaster exploded from the wall near his face. He ran from the room. Behind him the connecting door was opening wider, and as he stumbled through the hallway door, he fell to his knees, crawling. A bullet thudded in the wall directly in front of him.

He was on his hands and knees, crawling, scrambling across the hallway stone floor, trying to get back on his feet, to get out of the firing line. He shifted left, only to see a second assassin, leaning against the opposite wall beside the fire exit. This man was tall and powerfully built, his chest and upper arms creating odd puckers in the seams of his blazer. Stepping from the wall he put himself directly between Calder and the exit. "All right, professor," he said.

Calder did not stop scrambling. His right leg came underneath him, putting him into something like a sprinter's starting position.

His adversary looked up and down the hallway as he reached into his jacket, and as he did so, Calder sprang from the floor as from a starter's gun, his mind blank.

The assassin was two, perhaps three strides ahead of him. As Calder rose from the floor toward him, head down, arms outstretched, the man's fingers were closing around his gun, but Calder was upon him before he could clear the holster, dropping a shoulder into the center of his chest and driving him backwards through the door. The fire alarm blared, covering the sound of the assassin's gun which, still holstered, fired into his own chest. The metal fire door slammed shut behind them and Calder watched as the dead man fell backwards down the stairs. A moment later, the first assassin blasted through the door. Calder had just a moment to grab at his gun.

The two men tumbled down the concrete stairs, first one on top then the other. Calder extricated himself slightly as they fell over the last stair onto a little landing. He delivered a kick under the chin. The man caught Calder's leg and began to twist, but Calder kicked with his other foot, catching him on the ear. Calder braced himself against the metal handrail and drove his heel into the side of his attacker's knee. Screaming, the man countered with a fist in the side of Calder's face. The blow stunned Calder, and the man was upon him again, the blaring alarm covering the sound of their fighting.

In the stairwell, as the man drew back to smash Calder's face for the third time, Calder dimly wished someone would come down the stairs to escape the supposed fire. The fist hit him just below the temple, glancing across his eye and sending him into momentary darkness. The punch sent him reeling against the far wall, his knees giving out. In his darkness, as he struggled to remain on his feet, he grasped at the fire extinguisher in the corner to hold him up. Dark became dusk in his mind, and he turned slightly toward his assailant, who was reaching for the gun on the step above him. In one fluid movement, Calder unhooked the extinguisher from the wall and swung it wildly, hitting him on the side of the head.

Blood covered the landing and the wall where the skull had made contact. Calder swung the extinguisher again, catching the man in the jaw. There was a crunching sound and the assassin stopped moving. Calder took off down the stairs.

As Calder exploded through the fire escape door into the

lobby, he ran straight into the security guard who had let him in. The guard put his arms around Calder to slow him down.

"Jesus!" Calder screamed, "they've killed him. They tried to kill me."

"Who?" asked the guard. "Who?"

"Why didn't you come? The alarm was sounding. Why didn't you come?"

"Who? What's happened?"

"Two of them. They were shooting. They've killed Novaczeck. Hurry."

Outside, a fire truck drew up, making its routine response to a routine false alarm.

"Help them," cried Calder. "Go! Hurry! I'll be okay. Fifth floor."

The guard turned to run up the stairs, his pale blue shirt now stained with blood. Calder left by a side exit marked "Emergency Only." He found himself in high bushes from where he saw a police car pull up. Dully, the policeman stepped out of his car and looked around as the first firemen entered the building. In the rapidly fading light, the people gathering outside seemed to appear and disappear as the fire and police lights strobed. Calder became nauseated as he looked at the scene.

The policeman stood with one foot on the car sill, the other on the pavement as he talked into his radio, his dark skin turning orange, then blue and back to orange in the flashing light. He quit talking for a moment as he scanned the upper floors and then began again, shaking his head.

Calder backed away from the building, hunched over, dripping blood on his hands and pants. Rather than risk being seen, he ran across the street toward an alley behind another building, where he slowed to a trot.

The adrenaline rush was being replaced by a throbbing head. He spit blood every few steps. One of his teeth was loose. As he loped along, he kept his arms immobile near his body so as not to make the pain in his shoulders and arms any worse. As he crossed the next street and continued through the alley, he caught sight of himself in a blackened storefront window.

His right eye was swollen, almost closed. His lips were split and swollen, twisted by the extra blood filling them. The top of his left cheekbone looked as though it had been sand-papered. His right ear bled, as did a cut above his right eye. He stopped and looked at the reflection. With great effort, for his neck no longer seemed to turn, he twisted his head enough to examine his left side. Where the right side of his face was a jagged, lunar landscape, his left side had only minor scrapes, a slight swelling at his left cheek where his head had hit the wall.

The cold air bit at the tops of his ears, making them sting, but the cold was a mercy on his open wounds. Around his face and neck, the heat of so much blood so close to the surface created an odd umbra of warmth which had increased as he had slowed and stopped.

The rapidly falling darkness covered him; and the cold kept most people off the streets. He continued through the alley as fast as he could, walking quickly for five blocks, until he came to a wide avenue. Across the street was a park.

He doubled back, grateful for the absence of people in this commercial district in the early evening on a Saturday. Gradually he began to feel he was coming into possession of himself again. As the higher functions of his brain returned, he felt frustrated, childishly angry at his inability to see properly or to remember things he had passed. He turned around as he crossed each street, wondering how many blocks he had come. The light from the street lamps seemed to arc at him, shards of electric blue that stung at his mind.

A hunted animal again, his strength seemed to flow out of him with each step and each drop of blood. Then, across the way and glittering in the darkness, he saw a telephone stand. Not a lighted booth, but a freestanding payphone with a shell around it. He looked at his watch, but its face was smashed, too. He lingered over it, his mind blank.

As he approached the telephone stand, at an angle to keep the passing headlights from hurting his eyes, he pulled out the slip of paper Imogen have given him. How had the killers known about his meeting? He dialed the number.

The answering voice was Pakistani or East Indian. Calder asked for Imogen Trager. "Yes," said the man. "Imogen is here. Just a moment. Please hold the line."

There was silence for a moment, and Calder felt his consciousness flicker. His vision grew suddenly dim and contracted, like a computer screen going off.

"How'd it go?" asked Imogen brightly at the other end, and Calder snapped back.

"Novaczeck's dead," he said. "They were waiting for me."

"How? Are you okay?"

"No. I need help. I need you. Can you come get me?"

"Jesus, Duncan, what happened?"

"I . . . I can't think. It seemed . . . Come get me. Please."

He must have blacked out, for the next thing he knew, Imogen was lifting him away from the wall of the phone booth. He had not fallen, but he had no sense of the passage of time. As he stood, he noticed that the white plastic of the inner shell was smeared in browning blood.

"Duncan," she was saying. "Duncan?"

He limped to Imogen's car, leaning heavily on her. "I'm sorry," he said. "I'm sorry."

"You'll be all right now," she said soothingly, not because she believed it but because it seemed the proper thing to say.

"Safe now," Calder murmured.

Imogen did not feel safe now in the least. She wanted to

get away from Washington as quickly as possible. As she had driven over to get Duncan, she had held her purse between her thighs and rifled it for the key to her friends' house in Philadelphia. There it was, still inside the envelope in which it had come. "Thank God," she thought. "There isn't even a letter at home to betray me." Her assurance waned, though, as she realized she had no idea how they had found out about Duncan's appointment with Novaczeck. How could her office phone be tapped? she wondered.

By the time she was on the Beltway, heading for Interstate 95, Calder was breathing evenly and well and the bleeding seemed to have stopped. He looked awful, much worse than perhaps he was, she thought as she glanced again at his wounds. He might have a concussion, she thought. But he was talking and reasonably alert, so she resolved to wake him every hour or so until they reached Philadelphia. "Duncan," she said. "It's alright. We're going to Philadelphia. We'll be safe there. I think we'll be able to figure this out."

"Okay," Calder murmured without opening his eyes.

Fear suddenly burst through Imogen. "They will assume Calder is with me. They'd put out an APB to stop this car."

Imogen swerved, taking the first exit ramp she saw. At the bottom, she pulled over and stopped, grabbing her map out of the glove compartment.

Calder stirred. "What is it?" he asked. "Is this it?"

"No. Not yet. We're not out of D.C. yet. I'm worried about them looking for this car." Her mind raced. There was no way to rent a car without using a credit card. The police would be watching the airports and train stations. Imogen's mind raced. There were no back roads, no sufficiently deserted stretches of road along the I-95 corridor. She found the map and turned on the dome light. Annapolis!

She would have to risk the Beltway, she realized. There was no other way. But if she headed to Annapolis and over to

Delaware, north toward Wilmington and then approached Philadelphia from the New Jersey side, she could drive on relatively open road. She could even cross into Wilmington and come at Philadelphia from the west. But she would figure that out when she drew closer.

She returned to the Beltway and headed for Annapolis, taking care to drive the exact speed limit, drawing no unneeded attention. As she drove, she thought how fortunate it was she had had the car worked on only two months earlier. Her headlights were properly aimed; all the turn signals and brake lights worked. If she kept to the speed limit in such a common, anonymous car, there would be no reason for anyone to look twice at it, no reason to pull her over and run her plate; and on the two-lane highways through the Delaware farmland, there would be fewer police. Imogen breathed deeply, hoping the mere action of sighing would make her feel better. It didn't.

The night was clear and starry as they crossed into Delaware. The flat farmland spread on either side like an expanse of ocean. Imogen cracked her window for some fresh air. Amid the hum of the engine and the sound of the rushing wind and the cars, she slowly began to relax, only to have the fear rise again suddenly at the sight of a Delaware trooper by the side of the road. She glanced at her speedometer. Fifty-five exactly. She watched in her rearview mirror for the trooper to come up on her. Nothing happened, and she gradually relaxed again.

Duncan slept peacefully. If he had concussion, it was mild, for he seemed alert whenever she awoke him to check on him. His right eye was swollen shut now and the scrapes on his cheeks and above his eye were scabbing over, no longer sub-dermal pink, like newly born mice, but deeper, darker. He looked terrible, but she felt confident that he would recover.

At a little after nine o'clock, they passed through

Wilmington and into Pennsylvania. Duncan awoke some minutes later with a groan.

"My head," he said, touching his face gingerly.

"Almost there," said Imogen.

She drove slowly through the narrow streets of Queen Village, looking for Second and Catharine. She parked right opposite the row house belonging to the Anthropology Professor, just across from Mario Lanza Park. The house was new, its brick shiny and taller than the bricks in the older houses, but it wasn't conspicuous.

"Wait here," Imogen said. "And scrunch down in the seat a bit." She removed the key from the envelope and unlocked the front door. She stood there looking up and down the street. Seeing it was clear, she motioned for Duncan to come.

He drew himself out of the car with great effort and pain and limped across the street. She ushered him in the door and told him to sit at the kitchen counter.

"I'll be right back," she said, grabbing a set of keys from a kitchen drawer.

"Where's the bathroom?" asked Calder.

"Upstairs to the left."

She watched him stand and lumber up the stairs. Closing the front door, she went out the sliding glass back door to the garage, where she took the couple's car out and parked it on the street near where she had just parked hers. She then moved her own car to the garage and closed the door.

She sat a moment at the kitchen counter. Duncan was still in the bathroom. After ten minutes or so, she went upstairs and knocked on the door.

"You okay?"

"Getting cleaned up," he answered.

Imogen went into the bedroom next to the bathroom and turned on the television. She flipped through until she found an all-news network and sat down. Duncan came out of the bathroom, stripped to the waist, a damp hand towel to his right eye. The bruises on his back and ribs from tumbling down the stairs had begun to discolor.

With the dried blood off his face, neck and chest, he looked markedly better. Throughout the car trip, with his face and the front of his jacket covered in blood, lying so silently, Imogen had been unable to shake the image of him as a murdered corpse, like those black-and-white photos of Mafia hit victims. He sat on the edge of a chair next to the bed.

He was not a big man, perhaps five foot ten inches tall, with narrow hips, but there was strength. The muscles in his right shoulder rippled and flowed as he rotated the arm to get the stiffness out. His chest was taut, his stomach firm, his legs slender but solid. As he wiped the towel across his shoulders and the back of his neck, twisting and shaking his head to ease the stiffness, she had an image of him as he might have been when much younger: a delicate, almost pretty face; warm, green eyes looking out from under long, black lashes; a congenial aspect; a mouth quick and ready to smile.

In the warmth she felt for that bruised face, there was also the realization the face could change suddenly, too; and if it were not smiling at you, the potential for violence lurking within the body, stored in the shoulders and legs could be awful. In a rage, she felt, he would deal his blows and kicks with the precision of a thug. Calder finished wiping his neck and looked up at her. He smiled and the dark cloud hanging over her thoughts, as gray-purple as a bruise, vanished.

"Could you help for a second?" he asked. "I'm sure there's some hydrogen peroxide or alcohol, or something, but I can't see very well."

She rooted about the bathroom until she found some hydrogen peroxide, cotton balls and butterfly bandages.

"Is there a guest room?" he asked as she dabbed at the

cut above his eye.

She blew on the clean wound to help it dry as she tore open the bandage packet. "Yes," she said, pulling the adhesive strips off, "there is." She pasted the bandage gently across the cut. "But I think you should sleep down here with me." She rose on tiptoe and kissed the bandage above his eye.

"Okay," he sighed, with deep satisfaction. "Thank you. Thank you for everything."

Imogen was drawing away. Duncan slipped his right arm around her waist and pulled her tightly to him. They kissed.

Immediately he drew away, touching his lip. "Sorry," he said, smiling.

She ran her fingers through his hair.

"Um," he began, "tonight . . . I don't think—"

She smiled and drew him to her again.

Imogen climbed onto the bed, sitting up to watch the television. Duncan sat down on the edge of the bed next to her, his hand in back of him, resting on her thigh. The blood coursing through him, the heightened sensitivity it brought to his extremities would normally have been gorgeous and thrilling, but tonight it only pumped blood into his wounds and made more acute the throbbing aches and sharp pangs throughout his body. "I'm going to see if there's some aspirin or something," he said.

He opened the medicine cabinet, where some aspirin were buried behind other medications on the top shelf. He popped three into his mouth, turned on the water and slurped out of his hands to help wash them down. As he was drying his hands on the blood-soaked towel, he heard a news report beginning: "Our top story, the President's campaign manager, James Novaczeck, is dead, victim of a gang-style murder."

Duncan rushed back into the bedroom. Imogen stretched out her hand to him and he returned to his spot at the edge of the bed, closer to her than before, holding her hand.

"Details are still unclear at this time," the reporter on the scene began. "What we know is that a man entered the building at about seven o'clock this evening to see James Novaczeck, the president's campaign manager, and he is presumed to have been the last person to see Novaczeck alive. In addition, two other men was found dead at the scene."

Calder looked at Imogen. "I—," he said.

Imogen waved and said "Let me hear this."

"Police and investigators are making no comment about possible motives at this point, and we are unsure of the connection between Novaczeck and the unidentified dead men in the stairwell."

"This area of Washington is relatively quiet on a Saturday," continued the reporter, with little detail to report, "and the building itself was almost deserted. Novaczeck has been credited by many with much of the strategic planning that won Diane Redmond the presidency, and had worked previously on three other presidential campaigns. It is not known for sure that there was a political motive for the killing, which has come as a huge shock to the Democrats at their moment of victory."

"Here in Washington, there are more questions than answers."

President-elect Redmond read a statement regarding the death of her campaign manager, before the broadcast returned to the studio anchor with the second story of the day. "The Justice Department this morning released its findings regarding the allegations by the Republicans of voter fraud in Illinois. There was vote-tampering, it said, but no action would be taken. Regina Lawrence has more in Illinois."

So she had. "The Justice Department findings regarding James Christopher's fraud allegations leave many here frustrated." The screen cut to the U.S. Attorney for Northern Illinois, who read a prepared statement while standing next to the Illinois Attorney General. "After exhaustive review," the U.S. Attorney began, "we have found no reason to reverse the results of the election. Though there were possible irregularities, those irregularities existed on both—I must stress—on both sides, and the degree of tampering was not sufficient to overturn the result."

The report cut back to Regina Lawrence. "This is not the kind of thing people in Illinois wanted to hear—"

Imogen pressed mute on the remote.

"That was you, wasn't it?" said Duncan. "Your work?"

"Yes," said Imogen. "Was that you? What happened exactly? Start at the beginning. I dropped you off and you went up to Novaczeck's office. Then what?"

Calder related what he knew, about the two men. "He was reaching for his gun. I was dazed. I grabbed the fire extinguisher and swung. Hit him two or three times."

Imogen was staring at him, not knowing what to think.

They were silent.

"Duncan," said Imogen, "I'm scared. How could they have known about the meeting without tapping my Bureau phone? And that's almost impossible—"

"—unless you *are* the FBI." Duncan slid over to her on the bed and hugged her.

"Where do we go?" she asked. "Who do we trust?"

"I don't know."

CHAPTER THIRTEEN

Imogen awoke first, separated in the bed from Duncan. Their attempts to embrace in the night had resulted only in howls from him, as she put a knee wrong or inadvertently applied pressure somewhere acutely sensitive.

She went downstairs and put water on for coffee, then went out to the car for her laptop. Duncan came padding down the stairs as she settled herself at the kitchen counter, taking her first sip of coffee. He smiled at her and crossed to the sink, where he filled his hand with water to wash down some aspirin. Imogen poured him coffee. His hand trembled with weakness as he raised the cup to his lips. He touched the rim gingerly against his bottom lip before sipping.

The swelling in his lips had gone down considerably, but his right eye looked a disaster. Imogen realized he could not see through the swelling, and that his sudden head jerks were no more than attempts to see something that his other eye had glimpsed. He seemed to be looking askance at everything.

"I've only felt weaker and worse," he said as he set the cup down, "one other time in my life—freshman year at college. I drank most of a bottle of Everclear, cut with cherry Kool-Aid."

Imogen smiled and shuddered at the thought.

"That next morning, I thought I was going to die. This morning, I know I won't die, but I wish I could."

"We have work to do," said Imogen. "Maybe it'll take your mind off it."

"Yes. You're right. Mustn't grumble."

"Here's what I think," Imogen began. "We need help. We have to trust someone."

Duncan looked up at her warily through the good eye.

"I think you knew this was coming, Duncan. My boss, Pollack. We're desperate. We have to trust someone."

Calder nodded. "But why Pollack?" he said. "What can he help us with?"

"We're going to see the Attorney General," said Imogen.

"We are."

"Yes," she said.

"There's no way we could get in to see her," said Calder. "The FBI, the Secret Service, the D.C. police are all looking for me."

Imogen grunted her assent.

"Right," said Calder. "So there's no way I could get in. You, maybe; but never me unless—"

Imogen smiled.

"Could he . . . ?" Calder asked.

"He's the Executive Assistant Director."

"I know, but—"

"What did you tell me that time I forgot to register for that dissertation class in time? when I thought that because I'd forgotten, my funding would be gone, my student loans, and that I'd have to withdraw for the quarter? Do you remember what you said?"

"I said that every bureaucracy has its ironclad rules, but that within each bureaucracy, there is always someone who can bend those iron rules," he said, as though reciting a tiresome lesson.

Imogen beamed.

"So Pollack is that person," said Calder.

"One of them," said Imogen, not wanting to overstate her case.

"And with what will Pollack help us?"

Imogen poured more coffee for both of them. "Okay," she began, "Novaczeck was our last best hope. We figured he was untouchable; that he could take our information directly to the president. Well, now we see how long the conspirators' arm really is." She paused. "The plot will go through now. I don't see how we can stop it."

"I know," said Calder.

"But we're not dead yet—and we can do an end-run around anyone who wants to hush this up."

Calder straightened on his kitchen stool. "How?" he asked.

"We get Pollack to take us to the AG. Up until now, we've been correct in thinking that giving this to the press would make us sound like crazy conspiracy theorists. But with Novaczeck dead, everything we know becomes instantly credible."

"So we should get it out there now."

"No. Not yet. If we do it now, the conspiracy closes down, and any leads we have die. Now, the conspiracy goes ahead, which tips their hand, which gives us the chance to catch them. So, I tell Pollack as much as will get us in, impress upon him the need for secrecy. I tell him about you; that you are not the murderer; that you have vital information. With Novaczeck dead, our data will have instant credibility."

Imogen paused. "We'll be okay. If we're not safe inside the Justice Department with the Attorney General of the United States, there really is no hope. Yesterday, you said paranoia had taken you a long way. I am not abandoning that stance, so much as altering posture."

"That's a nice distinction," said Calder, smiling.

"I am attempting to help us get the information out."

"And you trust Pollack?"

"Implicitly," she said.

"And what about his talking to someone else?" said Calder, remembering the reason they had earlier decided against bringing him in.

"It's a chance we'll have to take. I'll make it clear to him the Department might be dirty. With Novaczeck's death, that will carry some weight."

"Someone might recognize my name when he gets the passes."

"I'll make sure he meets us at the security check." She paused a moment. "So far," she continued, "we have had to act as though everyone were in on this plot, because we could not risk the consequences of trusting and being wrong."

"Exactly," said Calder.

"But this morning, I thought of a slightly different tack. While it's true we cannot be sure who is doing this, and must act as though everyone we contact might be involved, it is safe to say there is no way everyone could be involved."

"Okay," said Calder.

"So," she said, "the trick now is how to broadcast message once we've told the Attorney General. If we get the information simultaneously to practically every White House reporter, we'll have covered ourselves. There is no way that every one of them is bent. I know the State Department, the CIA and FBI use journalists to get information all the time, but—"

"You've made your point," said Duncan. "It kills two birds. It gets the information out, and does it in a way that makes it impossible for anyone to cover it up." Calder sipped at his coffee. "Very good," he said admiringly.

"Let's get you some ice for that eye," said Imogen.

With Duncan now sitting beside her, a towel full of ice applied to his right eye, Imogen opened her laptop and began. "We'll abbreviate the summary somewhat," she said.

"And I think we want the names of those who were killed along with as many names of the replacements as we have."

"Good. That'll be at the end," said Imogen. "We'll get it down to two pages. I can shrink the type to make it fit, and then we'll make a hundred copies, double-sided. That way the reporters will have something easily held, something succinct. They have to take this seriously."

Duncan watched over her shoulder as she typed, her fingers flying across the keyboard. With only one eye to look through, however, staring at the screen was a disorienting and frustrating experience. He began to feel dizzy.

By about noon, they were satisfied with the phrasing of the summary. "We'll want to go to a copy center where I can print this out," said Imogen. "Do you have any money left?"

Duncan found fifty dollars.

"I think I should go alone. There is a chance you would be recognized. And with that shiner, you're bound to attract attention. People are bound to look at you. When I get back, we'll call Pollack."

"Good," said Duncan.

Imogen went upstairs and was about to begin putting on the clothes she had worn for the past three days. She threw her blouse down on the bed. "Duncan?" she called from the top of the stairs. "Where did you find that clean shirt?"

At the bottom of the stairs, he paused, breath caught in his throat. Imogen wore only panties and his T-shirt. As she leaned forward to look down at him, her hands pressed together at her knees, her red hair fell lustrous and thick past her face, softly framing the tenderness and intelligence of her deep blue eyes. Her thighs seemed impossibly long, rising steeply to ample hips. She smiled at him and flicked a strand of hair behind one ear. Duncan was struck with awe and gratitude as he considered the contrast between them: she, fluid, graceful, vital; he, brittle, awkward, life signs fading— the frog and the princess.

"Outside the guest room on the third floor," he said, thinking it all sounded so happily domestic.

He continued to look up at her. For two nights he had slept in the same bed as this magnificent woman, and he wasn't even sure what had happened.

She smiled and walked back to the bedroom.

After she left, Duncan went to soak in a bath. He let himself gently, painfully into the steaming water and lay back. Under the water, he gingerly massaged each affected area. In the heat, his head seemed to swell and throb. Visions of Imogen haunted him. As he closed his eyes and tried to relax, he imagined her again in the bath at the hotel, and then as she had been half an hour earlier, at the top of the stairs smiling at him. Within the benevolence and well-being which issued from that image, he felt a rising dread, too.

Suddenly, somehow, they were not alone. He saw her smiling there at the top of the stairs being suddenly grabbed from behind—saw the assassin from the stairwell take her by the shoulders and begin punching her. Her head recoiled as his own had with each punch in that struggle for life. The man's fist looked bigger, eclipsed her face. Her eye swelled and bled, her cheek bruised.

He opened his eyes, feeling sick to his stomach. He had not conjured that scene. It had burst upon him. His eyes open now, he recalled Novaczeck, with his chest exploded as if from within. He saw Matthew too, stiff and pale, body wet with dew by the side of the road. Despite the hot bath, Duncan felt cold inside. He could not let Imogen get hurt, he thought. It was his fault she was in this at all. He was resolved. If either of them were to come to any harm, it should be him. Her plan was a good one, but they would have to be very careful.

When Imogen returned, he was writing at the dining room table. Along with the leaflets she had copied, she brought in two Cheese-steak Sandwiches and a bag of cheese fries. "When in Rome," she said as she spread the food out on the table.

Duncan smiled.

"I've never felt like such foreigner in an American city

before," she said, biting into her sandwich. "I'm in line at Pat's Steaks about ten blocks from here," she continued, a strand of grilled onion resting on her chin, "and I'm listening to the people in front of me order. The first guy steps up and all he says is 'I'll have a Whiz wit'. The next man says he'll have 'a Provie wit'. Looking at the menu, I realized it was superfluous to say Cheese-steak Sandwich, since that was all you could buy, and that all they needed to know was what kind of cheese. So I, suddenly feeling quite the native, ordered two Provolones. The man at the window asks, 'wit?' He must have seen the glazed look in my eyes, because he said: 'wit onions or not?' So I got us two Provie wit.

"So, what's a Whiz wit?" asked Calder.

"Cheese Whiz with onions," she replied.

"That's disgusting."

Imogen shrugged.

"These are really good," said Calder as he tore ravenously at his sandwich.

With lunch finished, Duncan read through one of the leaflets with satisfaction.

"I should call Pollack soon," said Imogen.

"Yes. But before you do, though . . . I've been thinking. You need to be careful about what you tell him. Just enough information to get us in."

"Okay, Duncan. Is there something you're not telling me?"

In his mind's eye, Calder saw Imogen, crumpled on the floor, dying of a gunshot wound. "No," he said. "I just want to be careful. I want to be as close to the Attorney General as we can be."

"We should call from a payphone," she said. "There's an Irish pub four blocks from here. It's within a quarter mile of the freeway. Even if they know where the call came from, they won't have much to go on. They'll figure we could be anywhere, that we just got off the freeway, made the call and were gone. We can walk there."

"Good," he said.

The pub was almost empty in the early Sunday afternoon. They ordered at the bar, and Imogen asked about a payphone. The bartender, a tall, lanky man about forty years old, gestured toward the back, his arm so long it seemed to stretch almost to the hallway at which he pointed. Imogen asked for three dollars in change.

"Follow me in a minute or two," she said quietly to Duncan as she walked to the back. The bartender leaned forward over the bar to watch her walk away and smiled approvingly, but the smile disappeared in the next moment, when he caught sight of Calder. Caught out, he shrugged and went back to his inventory.

Imogen seated herself at a barstool next to the phone and dialed Pollack's cell.**

"Hi, Doug. It's Genny."

"Hi, Gen," he said. "What's up?"

"I need your help, Doug."

"Sure. What is it?"

"Who's working on the murder of Jim Novaczeck, the president's campaign manager?"

"Secret Service, I think. We're way out of that."

"No one in our Department?"

"No. He has to do with elections, obviously, but this isn't our turf."

"Actually, it is."

Pollack paused at the other end of the line. "And why is that?"

Calder arrived and leaned against the opposite wall.

"His death has everything to do with this election. Hear me all the way through."

"Okay."

"Tomorrow, a plot will play itself out, and the president-elect will lose the election."

"What? How?"

"I'm getting to that," said Imogen. "The man the police are looking for in connection with Jim's death is a Political Science professor. They're trying to locate him in connection with the murder because he has evidence that would stop the plot from happening. They have made two attempts on his life, one of them at Novaczeck's office."

"Who? I mean, who are you saying is plotting this?"

Imogen sighed. It was, she realized, too much to ask that he listen to the story all the way through.

"That's the problem," she said. "We're not sure. I set up a meeting between the professor and Novaczeck last night."

"You did? Why didn't you come to me right away?"

"Hear me out. You remember I was seconded to Novaczeck? So I had his number. I made the arrangement for the professor, but two men were waiting for him when he got there. There's no way they could have known unless they tapped my phone, at the Bureau, which is the number I told Novaczeck to call. Presumably the only person who could tap an FBI phone would have to be *be* FBI, Justice, CIA or NSA."

"So you know this professor? the guy in the building the police are after?"

"Duncan Calder, yes. He was my graduate advisor."

"Where is he now, Imogen?"

"He's standing right next to me."

"And where are you?"

"I can't say, Doug."

"Is he—clear your throat if there's a problem."

"I have not been abducted, Doug. I came to pick him up after he was almost killed. I drove the car."

"Jesus, Gen, do you know how serious this is? You could go to jail . . . you could be fired." Imogen rolled her eyes. In Pollack's worldview to be fired was much worse than jail.

"Doug, I think someone in the Department is dirty. I know it isn't you, but I won't—I can't—come in until I am sure it's safe. I will not go to jail. If what I want to do works, you and I will get commendations. I have a plan."

"Genny. Imogen."

"I did not plan to get into this, Doug. But I'm in it now. I think we're safe for the time being. But we have been followed almost everywhere we've gone. Whoever these people are, they can tap FBI phones. Duncan has been beaten and shot at. The conspiracy is operating on a national level. They tailed him here from Seattle, and there's other stuff going on. To do with the election. You are my only hope of getting the information to the Attorney General."

"You want to meet with the Attorney General?"

"The election is about to be stolen and she may be the only person who can stop it."

"So what is happening, Gen?"

"I have evidence that a series of Electors have been murdered, their murders made to look like accidents, and no one is following up because each case is being dealt on the local level. That's all I want to say right now, Doug. What I need is two passes to get us into a meeting with the AG."

"You're out of your mind, Gen!"

"Doug, this is the best way. We have to let the these people play their hand to get them in the open, and we need to get the information out in such a way as to make sure no one in the administration can cover up what's going on. This is big. It's the kind of thing that might be covered up. And if we merely root out those directly involved, we'll never get hold of the ones in charge, and there will be nothing to stop them the next time."

"Can the Bureau be hurt by this?" asked Pollack.

"Only the few who are in on the plot," said Imogen. "I don't think it's systemic to the Justice Department."

"So—" said Pollack pausing to think. "Okay," he began,

"let me get this straight: I'm supposed to get you two passes to a meeting with the Attorney General."

"Correct."

"And one of the passes is to be given to a suspect in a murder; and this suspect is to be granted access to the Attorney General of the United States. Presumably, I'm not to tell anyone what little I know?"

"How can I convince you?" said Imogen.

"You can start by being straight with me! That's how."

Imogen took a deep breath. "Even given all that I have said about my distrust of the Department, my concern over cover-ups, the breadth of this conspiracy, their boldness—even with all that, I'm trusting you. I trust your honor and integrity; I trust your patriotism. I know you cannot be bought. I would hope you think the same of me."

"Yes, Gen, I do . . . Look: come in now. We'll protect you. I'll handpick the people."

"No, Doug. You can't guarantee to protect us. No one can. We have not been safe, and we won't be safe until the plot is fully revealed and the conspirators are in jail or on the run."

"But—"

"What half measure would you accept, Doug?" Imogen waved at Duncan who had begun pacing up and down the hallway in front of the bathrooms.

"I need to know what the hell is going on!" yelled Pollack.

Imogen waved furiously at Duncan. "Just a minute," she said to Pollack. Calder quit pacing and walked over to Imogen. She picked up a pen and began writing on the notepad on a shelf below the payphone. Quickly, she scrawled: "meet w/ Pollack to brief?"

Calder wrote: "Meet at —? brief inside—before AG if necess. But INSIDE." He underlined the last word twice.

Imogen thought for a moment. "Doug," she said, "you

get us in. Once inside, somewhere safe, we will show you the data we've been working on, tell you everything we know. If it doesn't make sense . . . if you don't believe it—"

"—You know I want to help you. More than I would someone else. But try to see it from my side: if someone came to you with this—"

"That's just it, Doug," said Imogen, her voice a harsh, rasping whisper. "I am not just someone. I am an agent of the United States' Federal Bureau of Investigations. I am an expert in elections and voter fraud. Have I ever been wrong?"

"No, that's true, you—"

"And right now I am telling you that the person who taught me everything I know has information about something huge, something sinister, the kind of thing for which the Justice Department exists! I have checked his data personally, and I am telling you that there has been not just corruption but murder."

"—Imogen—"

"This is why there is an FBI, Doug."

At the other end of the line, Pollack was silent.

When Imogen spoke again, she was calm, composed, matter-of-fact. "Doug," she said. "Tomorrow, all hell is going to break loose politically, and we—Duncan and I— have the evidence to stop it going any further. I won't be at work tomorrow. Even the Bureau isn't safe. I'm going to call you tomorrow at about—" she looked to Duncan "—four—" she said, arching her eyebrows at Duncan, asking if that was good time; he shrugged his agreement "—or four-thirty—to agree where and when we can meet."

"Gen, I can't do this. I won't. There's nothing I can do until I have something concrete from you."

Imogen stared at the floor, defeated. Her mind raced for another reason, another way to convince Pollack.

"Doug, I'll call you tomorrow at four. By then you'll have all the concrete reasons you need to get us in."

"I'll be waiting for your call, Gen."

"Thank you Doug. Talk to you tomorrow." Imogen hung up the telephone and sighed deeply.

Back inside the house, Imogen fell heavily backward against the front door to close it. "How do criminals do it?" she asked Duncan. "This is exhausting."

"I've thought the same thing," he said.

"But we've done it, haven't we? All we do now is wait."

"Thanks to you," said Calder. "Yes."

She let her overcoat fall to the floor. "This is ridiculous," she said walking away from the coat. Duncan picked it up, put it on a hanger and hung it next to his in the hallway closet.

Imogen looked behind her at Calder as she started up the stairs. "I think you should come upstairs with me," she said. "Now."

Upstairs, she sat Calder down on the bed. She bent down and delicately kissed the scar over his right eye. She took his chin gently in her hand and tipped his head up to her.

Slowly, she lowered her mouth to his. Duncan's body became tense, as though preparing for a shock of pain. Her lips closed gently, tentatively on his upper lip. But there was no pain. His tension melted instantly and he reached up with his right hand to cup the back of her head. He pulled her firmly to him.

She lowered herself onto his lap, straddling him, her knees on the edge of the bed either side of his hips. For a moment, they held one another, he resting the left side of his face gently on her chest, his arms closed firmly across her back. She stroked his thick, black hair. In the rush of heat coursing through them, each felt the need to flex toward the other, felt the aching need to stretch and strain their bodies, as though just having arisen from a long slumber.

Duncan's skin felt coarse and hot. It longed to press,

unfettered, against the supple smoothness of her arms, the yielding softness of her breasts. He opened his palms and ran them up toward her shoulders, his forearms pressing against her back.

She felt the muscles in his broad shoulders flex and roll as his hands worked their way up. She breathed deeply the scent of his hair, took a firm grasp of a clump of it and squeezed it between her fingers. Then she took Calder by the shoulders and slowly pushed him down on the bed onto his back. She rose over him, knees still astride, and pulled off the sweater and T-shirt she was wearing. She unhooked her bra and let the straps slide off over her arms.

Below her, Duncan struggled out his shirt. His back arched involuntarily; his chest ached out to her. He clasped her smooth shoulders and drew her down to him. They had both been waiting for this, imagining it. As they embraced, their skin yielding to one another's, they both drew breath hungrily, as though together they had just broken the surface after a deep dive.

At Headquarters, Pollack could not shake his misgivings about what Imogen had told him, but he was going to be ready nevertheless. He was rifling his secretary's desk. "Goddamnit," he hissed as he slammed another file drawer shut. "How many fucking forms are there?!" He crossed quickly to the file cabinet facing his secretary's desk and threw open the top drawer. He gave a cursory glance at the files and forms in the top drawer and slammed it shut. He stalked into his own office, to look up his secretary's home number.

"Come on, come on," he said as the phone rang at the other end.

"Hello?"

"Sharon. It's Doug Pollack. Listen, I'm sorry to bother you at home, but I'm here at work and something's come up.

Where are those forms for emergency clearance?"

"Clearance for what?"

"Security clearance. Something that might get a civilian in to see the AG."

"It's in your office," she said patiently. "Third drawer down, but it's locked. Do you have the key?"

"Oh, okay. I didn't think to look there. Hold the phone a sec, would you?"

"Okay," she said.

Pollack fumbled with his keys and opened the drawer. After a moment or two, he found it. He went back to the phone. "Okay," he said, "Got them. Thanks. Now, what do I do?"

"You need one form for each person, and it must be countersigned. Anyone with TS clearance."

"Okay. Thanks, Sharon. And again, sorry to bother you on a Sunday."

"That's fine. See you tomorrow." And she hung up.

Tom Kurtz knocked on the outer door.

"Doug?" he said.

"Yeah," answered Pollack.

Kurtz came into the room, a security guard tagging behind. "Jesus," he said. "You had me worried. I heard all this banging around—" Kurtz turned to the security guard. "Sorry, Ted, false alarm."

The security guard shrugged and walked out.

"Sorry to find you in here on a Sunday as well."

Kurtz looked terrible. He was haggard, his suit rumpled as though he had slept in it, his hair unkempt. "What are you doing here, Doug?" he asked.

"Something's come up," answered Pollack, wondering what he should say beyond that. Imogen's paranoia had gotten under his skin, though he was feeling much calmer now that he was inside the Bureau.

His anxiety subsiding, Pollack again felt himself

bristling at the suggestion that anyone in his Bureau might be other than loyal. Here, for instance, was Kurtz. Hard at work on a Sunday, doing his job, meticulously, anonymously, protecting the rights and interests of the country. The idea that anyone in the Bureau could be dirty made Pollack angry. Maybe Imogen had reason to believe it, but she had not worked at the FBI as long as he had. When this was all over, he was going to have to talk to her.

"What's kept you here, Tom?" asked Pollack.

"This Illinois thing," answered Kurtz.

"That's over and gone, isn't it?"

"Yes and no," replied Kurtz. "I don't like it. I don't like the way we handled it. I think we gave away too much. We should have just given it a clean bill of health and been done with it. The public has difficulty with complexity. I've said this before."

"Yes," said Pollack. "You have."

"I know we disagree."

"Tom, we don't so much disagree, as I dislike you wasting energy second-guessing decisions made higher up."

"But they're wrong. The public doesn't want to know. They want simplicity. They want right or wrong. Good or bad. Simple. I think it was a big mistake to tell them that both parties were engaged in fraud in Illinois. Our doing nothing about it leaves an unsavory taste in people's mouths."

"What are you saying?" asked Pollack.

"We are the FBI, part of the Justice Department. We did not deal justice; we said, 'Oh well, because both did it, there's nothing we can do'."

"Well, that's not what we reported. We noted that while—"

"Doug, truth is like Genny's statistics work: most people can't understand it, and they resent it."

"Well, that was the deal: we got to divulge everything we knew—got to be seen as the cavalry riding in to save the

182

day—and in exchange, we let the locals clean their own house. It was as much a political decision as a decision between—"

"—And that's the problem, Doug. It looks like a political decision. Justice should be seen as above that; should at least appear to be blind. It should be swift and clear. We may make political choices, but we cannot be seen to have done so." Kurtz calmed himself. "Anyway, I was going over my notes, my findings."

"All weekend?"

"—um, no. No. I was out late . . . I got it into my head to come in. You know."

Pollack nodded. "Close the door and come in then," said Pollack.

Pollack seated himself behind his desk, Kurtz in a chair facing him. "I need your help," Pollack began.

"Anything I can do."

"Something's about to happen . . . it may have to do with this Illinois thing, but whatever it is, apparently there's a plot to change the election outcome."

"How?"

"I'm not sure. I'm working pretty much in the dark. And I'm going to ask you to do something without much to back it up, but we need to prepared."

"Okay," he said guardedly.

"It's nothing illegal," said Pollack, "and I will take full responsibility. As you are directly under me, and acting under my orders, if this all goes south on us, you will be covered. I take whatever fall there may be to take." As he said these words, Pollack worked mentally through the logistics of getting Imogen and Calder in; and he would not let them past him until he was fully satisfied with their evidence.

Kurtz hesitated. Then, calmly, he asked Pollack: "What are you talking about?"

Pollack wasn't sure what he was going to say, but began. "I have promised absolute secrecy, but I can't do it alone. I need you."

"I'm with you," said Kurtz. "So, what is it, and what is going to happen?"

"Imogen called," said Pollack. "She's in trouble, and needs help." And he related what little she had told him and what she had asked.

"Do you believe her?" asked Kurtz.

"Apparently, we'll have the proof late tomorrow, and I'm not going to tell her I'm going through with this until then. I have promised her absolute secrecy on this. It's going to be just us three. I'm to get her and this professor in to see the AG."

"She said nothing more?"

"That's all I have to go on. But Lord knows, Gen isn't someone to go off half-cocked. She's not a conspiracy theorist. I'm taking this a little on faith."

"Sounds like you're taking it a lot on faith," said Kurtz.

"You would go about it differently?" asked Pollack "I want your view."

"Okay," said Kurtz, "when she calls, I say we trace on the call. We demand she tell us where she is or it's no deal. We demand she let us come get her. If she really is in the danger she says, she and the professor will need our protection."

"She says she doesn't believe we can protect her."

"That's bullshit," said Kurtz. "Fucking melodrama."

Pollack nodded. "If it were just Gen, I'm sure we could get her to come in, but the real question mark is this professor. We know almost nothing about him."

"And she knew him before?" asked Kurtz.

"Quite well. He taught her."

"And you think he's behind the unwillingness to be reasonable. Because that's what she's being: unreasonable."

184

"It's possible," said Pollack.

"Okay," said Kurtz. "We trace the call tomorrow. She can't be too far. We could have agents there in no time. I'll oversee it myself."

"She's bound to have thought of that, Tom."

"Damn!" said Kurtz. "I wish we knew where she was. I'm worried about her. Her safety...her sanity."

"Me, too," said Pollack. "Anyway, let's keep it quiet but get it rolling. I need you to sign this emergency clearance for both of them. But let's be clear, they are not going anywhere near anyone until we know what's going on."

"Agreed," said Kurtz, pausing before he signed. "I want to be on point for this, Doug," he said. "I want an APB out for Imogen and Calder. I want to be the one ready to go get them if they're spotted." He paused. "I don't know if you know this, but Imogen and I—"

"Everyone knows, Tom."

"Well, then you know, the thought of her being mixed up in something like this, at large with a suspected killer. I don't like it."

"I think we should do it her way," said Pollack.

"Let me put out the APB," begged Kurtz.

"No," said Pollack. "It might screw things up when they get close. If Genny's right about this, that'll be the most dangerous place for them. No APB."

"You want my views, but you won't listen to them," said Kurtz.

"I'm sorry, Tom. Not on that."

Shaking his head, Tom Kurtz signed the emergency clearance for Imogen. "I say we take them in through the parking garage," he said, adding his name to the order for Calder.

"Then that's how we'll do it," said Pollack, who had thought to bring them in through the front but wanted to make some concession.

185

"And," said Kurtz, "I want to be there."
"Okay, Tom."

CHAPTER FOURTEEN

December 19, 2016

Duncan could not remember having felt so relaxed in his life. They had made love throughout the afternoon and into the evening. Their exertions had sent them to sleep at about ten o'clock and the night had been utterly carefree, as though their passion for one another had created a cocoon of safety about them. The bed had seemed for a time to be its own benevolent country, the lands and peoples beyond its borders uninteresting and barbaric.

Duncan left Imogen sleeping and went down to make the coffee. Upon his return, he set the pot and cups on a table by the television and turned to look at her. A white, diffuse morning light poured through the windows, dazzled across the white sheets, washing out Imogen's pale features, accentuating the redness of her hair. The faint blond streak running from her crown past her temple was almost white.

Duncan felt mute in the face of such perfection, imagined himself small and hideous by comparison. He felt like some crude magnate who had drunk deeply of a magnificent wine which few but he could afford, but which he lacked the palate to fully appreciate. He gazed at each detail of her, but she stirred and the moment was gone. And what came next was still better.

She blinked in the bright light as she sat up in bed to face him and smiled.

"How long have you been standing there?" she asked.

"Not long. There's coffee."

"Ummm," she said, stretching.

Duncan poured and took the cup to her.

He had hurried as he ground the beans and poured them

into the pot. Having been raised in the West and worked all his life there, he was accustomed to news happening early. In his mind, he was three hours behind, as the Pacific Time Zone was three hours behind the Eastern.

It had not been until he set down the pot and cups, wondering where the television remote was, that he realized he was early; that there were no outposts to the nation ahead of the Eastern time zone. It was seven o'clock in the morning, and not only was he not behind, he had a very long day ahead of him and nothing had yet happened. He handed Imogen her coffee and slid under the covers with her.

They spent much of the morning in bed, until both of them, sated, rose and ranged about the house. In the living room, Duncan found an all-news radio station, and Imogen turned the television way up so she could hear it up in the third floor study. Duncan borrowed her laptop. He isolated the Democratic states, those which had a popular plurality for the President, the Democratic candidate, and highlighted the five in which someone would switch to the Republican: Maine, Massachusetts, Iowa, Washington and Oregon. Next to each, he typed the name of the original Elector, then a dash and that of the alternate, Faithless Elector.

He assumed there would be no special report until around 2p.m. Although there were seven who would switch, only three were needed to change the outcome of the election. The third switched vote would be in Iowa, in the Central Time Zone. If there were just two switched votes, it would merit only a spot on the evening news, but if the whole presidential race was overturned by the Electors' meeting at the Iowa state capitol in Des Moines, presumably no later than noon Central time, the news would be wall to wall. The Western states of Washington and Oregon would merely heighten the scandal for the evening news.

Imogen ordered pizza, which arrived at one o'clock. At two, as they hovered in front of the television in the bedroom, there was nothing but football recaps from the previous day and the routine headlines. At three o'clock they both began to feel sick. Duncan found himself unable to look Imogen in the eye.

At 3.30, East Coast time, CNN broke into its regular broadcast. Duncan popped open the screen of the laptop so he could check the reports against Matthew's data as the results came in. "I can't believe I'm looking forward to hearing this."

"I know," said Imogen.

The camera glanced to an anchor-woman: "This just in" she said. "We are just hearing that the result of the presidential election has been reversed. It appears Diane Redmond will *not* be the next President of the United States. The Presidency has been won by James Christopher, the Republican candidate."

"The closest election in recent history—decided on just four Electoral votes—has been reversed in the last half-hour by Electors voting in their state capitols. Unexpectedly, Democrat Electors casting their votes for President in New Hampshire, Minnesota and Colorado have voted for Christopher, swinging the election to the Republican at the very last moment. We go first to Concord, New Hampshire."

"What the fuck?" shouted Duncan. "New Hamp-shire?"

Imogen shushed Calder as the television cut to Concord.

"New Hampshire had a Democratic plurality, it's true . . . but no Elector died in New Hampshire," Duncan began. Imogen waved her hand at him, telling him to be quiet.

"Today in New Hampshire," the reporter began, "an Elector meeting in Concord began a trend which saw the reversal of the presumed outcome of the closest Presidential election in recent history."

A middle-aged man gazed about uncomfortably, his eyes looking beyond and above the intruding local TV camera. "It was an act of conscience. An individual act of conscience . . .

189

mine. I am a Democrat. I have always been a Democrat. But I am an American first. I do not believe the Justice Department's lies about the voting improprieties in Illinois. And so, as a protest, I cast my vote for the man I believe in my soul actually won the election: James Christopher. That's all I have to say."

The next report was from St. Paul, also by a local affiliate. "I have worked for the Democratic party since I was old enough to vote," one of the Electors said into the microphone. "I am a Democrat," he said nervously. "But I am an American, too. An American first of all. I love this country, and I believe in its capacity to rise above all. I believe in the Framers' built-in conscience of checks and balances. The election was stolen in Illinois, so I have cast my vote for James Christopher. I am at peace. God give me strength, God grant that I have done right." And he stepped away.

Calder stared at his data on the laptop screen as though it had betrayed him. "Minnesota was a Democratic state, too, but—"

In Denver, a well-dressed woman stepped up to speak to the nation. "In answer to your questions," she began, "No. No, I did not know that mine would be a decisive vote reversing the election. How could I have known? I . . . I acted for the right reasons. I did what I did as an act of conscience. No one should steal an election and get away with it. That was the message I meant to send, and . . . and since . . . and though it has reversed the outcome, I stand by my decision."

Imogen stood and walked out of the room. Duncan looked from her laptop to the television, and toward the open door. He wanted her back. He couldn't have her walk out like that. He heard the toilet flush. Moments later, she walked back into the room.

"We weren't wrong about the outcome," she said, standing at the door, "but we must have been wrong about the means."

Duncan nodded his head and looked back down at the little screen. "We were wrong," he said, as the data scrolled past. An idea occurred to him. "So fucking stupid," he hissed. He paused a moment and then began again. "Do you remember, there was a paper on drug policy that I suggested you use for your dissertation?"

Imogen shrugged.

"It turned out you didn't need it, but it used one obvious fact. I called it the don't-shit-where-you-eat effect?"

"Oh my God," said Imogen.

"Right: when the DEA is looking for a big drug port, they don't look at where there's a huge supply sold on the street, they look for a port city where there is virtually none to be bought."

"Because," Imogen chimed in, "you draw attention to yourself and your operation if you sell where you dock."

"Exactly. I was stupid," he said. "The replacements can't be plants. That would be too obvious, too easily found out, too clear a link. The replacements are just what they seem to be."

"Replacements," said Imogen. "It's like a shell game: look for where there is no action."

"Exactly."

"They're buying people all over. The dead ones were people who wouldn't switch their vote."

Duncan nodded. "It'll be harder to prove, but we still have the goods."

"Something to lean on them with," said Imogen, sounding again like an FBI Agent. "Our evidence doesn't get convictions, but it does get confessions; and confessions get convictions."

"Call Pollack," said Calder.

Imogen crawled across the bed to get at her clothes. On her way, she stopped to kiss Duncan. She went out of the house and down to the pub she had used to call Pollack before.

"Thank God you've called," said Pollack, picking up on the second ring. "You know what this is about? You can fix this?"

"Do we have the deal?

"Yes, White House access."

"White House access?" said Imogen

"I'll send a fucking helicopter to get you, land it on the damn roof if you think you can straighten this out," said Pollack.

"That won't be necessary, Doug. But why the White House?"

"This is all unprecedented. The president is calling a press conference, and he'll have the AG, the Speaker, Redmond and Christopher—all of them in the White House briefing room. Tell me you can help, Gen. You've got evidence of a plot?"

"Circumstantial evidence, Doug. But enough." Imogen glanced at the clock beside the bar.

"This is a plot? These Electors?"

"Yes. What time is the press conference?" Imogen asked.

"Nine o'clock tonight."

"Tonight?" Imogen looked at her watch. It was just after four. She calculated quickly. It would take her and Duncan half an hour to be ready to leave, rush-hour traffic for the first hour or so of driving. The earliest she could be back in Washington was eight p.m. "Ok," she said. "Eight p.m."

"Genny, if you could get here earlier…"

"Let's stick to the plan," she rejoined. "And part of that plan is keeping it quiet until it's too late. Okay?"

"Yeah. OK. I have the passes. I have everything ready.

Show your I.D. to the guard at the underground parking lot next to the Eisenhower Office Building. Your name is on the list, with an additional person of interest."

"Thank you, Doug. I knew you wouldn't let us down. I knew."

"I'll see you at the Eisenhower building entrance at?"

"Eight," said Imogen. "Maybe a little after." She hung up.

In Washington, Pollack hung up and looked across his desk at Kurtz.

Kurtz's face was white with anger and frustration. "It's in Philadelphia," he said.

"That's a big help," said Pollack sarcastically.

"I'm going to check every hotel in Philadelphia," said Kurtz impetuously.

"No, you're not," said Pollack distantly, his eyes fixed on a point through Kurtz. It was at least a three-hour drive, he calculated. Which was cutting it all a bit close.

Pollack was looking at the angles. He was getting calls from the press; calls, texts and memos from Public Integrity with questions about Imogen's findings in Illinois, calls from the US Attorney's Office, from the Bureau's Deputy Director. The Bureau had initiated a full-field investigation into corruption of the Illinois results and he was having to supply agents and staff. Subpoenas were flying. Pollack had a well-earned reputation for clear-eyed decisiveness, an ability to cut through the noise and deploy the right people in the right place with the proper instructions and mandate. But this was uncertain terrain, made worse because he felt sure he was missing something, felt uncertain about whom he could trust.

Imogen jogged back to the house and got Calder moving.

"You drive," she said as she pulled the front door of the house shut. She tossed him the keys to the anthropologist's

193

Acura, which would be safer for the trip back to Washington rather than risk being spotted on the road in her car. Troopers in the various states they would pass through might still be looking for her car.

"I need to work on something for Pollack," she said, settling into the passenger seat as they drove off.

"What is it?" asked Calder as they headed south.

Imogen popped open her laptop. "I'm writing something up for him to pass along. There's a writer for the *Post*, Jeff Callahan. I think he would be the best person to bring in, but it's Pollack who should send it. I'll spend a few minutes with a summary to orient him, but I won't send the email until we're about to go into the parking garage."

They drove in silence for much of the first two hours.

Duncan was thinking about the difference between how he had felt going to see Novaczeck only two days earlier and how he felt now. Then, on his way to see the President-elect's campaign manager, he had had the sensation of a clean break, an opening that would allow him to rush into the daylight out of this nightmare. He had seen a finish, an end. Despite misgivings about how his information might be handled by professional politicians, he had dared to think about what might lie beyond the end. Today, he was blank.

It was as though he were running from something, hunted and despised. Scared out of his wits, he was about to take a door that had been conveniently thrown open by Pollack. But he knew he would also have to find a way to survive going through, because his life would never be the same.

Imogen's emotions vacillated between feeling relief at coming to the end, and dread at what might be waiting for them. She trusted Pollack, but what if that trust was misplaced? What if she was walking Duncan into a trap again, as she had with Novaczeck? She also found herself wondering where she and Duncan would go from here, after today.

"So," Calder said, now continuing his thought process aloud, "like we talked about--when we get there, I think we should quickly but discreetly distance ourselves from one another."

"Jesus, Duncan. It's a press conference."

"Does the name Jack Ruby have any meaning for you?"

She did not like it, but she saw the sense.

"If something bad does happen, one of us has to run to the nearest camera, the nearest reporter, and start telling what we know: that the three Faithless Electors are not acting out of conscience but are part of a conspiracy to steal the presidency; a conspiracy that has already killed seven Electors across the country; and we have their names. *And we have evidence the seven deaths across different parts of the country were the first steps in a conspiracy to overturn the true result of the election. That will finish them.*"

Traffic slowed to a crawl as they drew near to the Eisenhower Executive Building. Three blocks from the White House, traffic was almost at a standstill. Imogen glanced at the clock: 7:20. Ten minutes later, near the entrance to the underground parking lot adjacent to the Eisenhower Executive Building, Imogen told Calder to go around everyone and into oncoming traffic along 17th Street for the final thirty yards to the garage entrance.

"What do you think you're doing?" demanded the guard, coming out of his kiosk. Imogen leaned across Calder and flashed her I.D. card. "Agent Trager," she said. "Imogen Trager. I am to be admitted by order of Douglas Pollack, Assistant Director."

"Yeah, I got it. Right here," said the guard taking down a clipboard. "Card," he said, holding out his hand. As he wrote some numbers down next to her name on the clipboard, she clicked 'send' on her laptop. The guard checked his watch and then wrote down the time. He handed her back the card.

"Park at the bottom level," he said. "Section A. You want the East stairs. The door will say E-six."

As they drove away, the guard signaled the next car in line to wait. He went to the kiosk, picked up the telephone and dialed a number. "Agent Kurtz?" he said. "Yes. They've just driven in. Yes, they're together." The guard listened a moment. "Yes," he said, "exactly where you told me to have them park. All right. Yeah, you're welcome," he said and hung up.

"I don't like this," Imogen said to Duncan as they wound their way down the spiral ramp toward the bottom level six flights below.

"No," Calder agreed.

The unease that Imogen so often felt in parking garages swept over her, but this was worse, as though they were being sent down a deep hole to be buried. When they arrived at the lowest level it was almost empty. Calder drove to the section where she had been directed. "Park as near to those cars as you can," she said. Calder was driving tentatively, constantly evaluating her position.

It struck her that their reactions had become primitive, animal-like. They never entered a building without sizing it up, never willingly went anywhere that was not well-lit and crowded. It seemed absolutely natural to her to eschew the wide expanse of empty lot in favor of a more crowded area.

Four cars were parked where Sections A and B abutted. Calder drove slowly past, allowing Imogen to look into and around them. He parked at the end of the line. "Not exactly Section A," he said.

Imogen approved of this tiny defiance, though she could not have explained its purpose either.

Six levels above them, Pollack stood inside the door to the garage, staring at a sparse group of reporters still trying to get into the White House. A harsh December wind whipped across the south lawn.

Pollack's phone vibrated. He checked it and saw the email from Imogen: "Doug, coming into the garage now. This is the evidence; I think it should also go to Callahan at the *Post* (his email is below). He'll be able to understand it, parse it. And with his knowledge and expertise, the others will report the way he frames it."

Pollack shook his head as he looked at the phone. He didn't have time to review the document. He hadn't even told Kurtz what little he knew. Novaczeck's death implied possible complicity at any level of government. He had been as evasive as he could be with the Secret Service—"two persons of interest to see the Attorney General." He wondered if he should be worried that it was Secret Service and not his FBI that was guarding the perimeter, but had seen no way around it. Bennett was the Secret Service agent in control of the site, he noted. At least Bennett was someone who had been around a long time, thought Pollack. Then he wondered whether longevity was good or bad under the current circumstances, a mixture of trepidation and rage growing within him.

Pollack looked at the email from Imogen again. Pollack wasn't sending anything until he had spoken to Imogen, and he certainly wasn't about to involve a reporter until he knew more.

Pollack looked at his watch, 7:35p.m. He cursed himself for not having been more proactive about protection. He'd have had them by now and would know they were safe.

Portable floodlights shined starkly on the scene at the White House west gate entrance along Executive Avenue, as Pollack looked out. He was accustomed at such times to feeling superior to the reporters. Usually, he, or someone who worked for him, was the source of the news, had the information for the reporters to disseminate. Today, he was no better than they; knew no more than they. Pollack's mouth twisted bitterly.

Imogen and Duncan were sick with worry. Duncan wondered if he should run, wondered if he should walk. He wondered where they could run to if they had to escape.

"I'll leave the car unlocked," said Imogen as she stepped out of the car and slammed the door shut. In the vacant garage, the sound reverberated, the report altered and hollow, from many directions at once. Calder felt himself jump at the sound, as he had jumped at the sound of a metal door slamming somewhere within the building in Gowen Hall that night, a lifetime ago, back in Seattle. The door he had to walk through was directly ahead: a heavy, gunmetal gray door marked E6.

Calder reached for Imogen's hand. When she took it, he realized they were both trembling. She squeezed his hand firmly and he pressed back. They paused to look at each other, and he knew as surely as if she had said it that she would do whatever was necessary. There was a sad strength in her eyes, as though she could see the future and did not like what she saw. As he squeezed her hand again, the trembling was gone.

The door burst open. Genny and Duncan involuntarily stepped backward.

Tom Kurtz walked through. "Thank God you're here," he said.

Imogen took another step back. "Tom?" she said.

Kurtz walked toward her, his arms wide as though to embrace her. "Pollack brought me in," he said. "He had to. Your passes had to be countersigned."

Seeing that Imogen was in full possession of herself and in no need of comfort from him, Kurtz dropped his arms to his sides.

"Professor Calder, I presume?" he said, holding out his hand, his smile genuine and warm. "Special Agent Tom Kurtz."

Duncan glanced at Imogen quickly before taking Kurtz's hand.

"Yes," he said. "Where do we meet Mr. Pollack?"

"Upstairs. I didn't want you using the elevators. Too hard to control. After what Pollack told me—"

"What did Pollack tell you?" asked Imogen.

"Damn little. Just that you've had a hell of a time. Professor, we'll expect you to cooperate fully with us in the investigation of Novaczeck's murder. After all this is done."

"Of course," said Calder stiffly. "But I think you'll find that everything will come clear, including Novaczeck's murder."

"I see," said Kurtz. "Two birds with one stone, so to speak?"

"Something like that." Calder hung back a moment, finding something false in Kurtz's familiarity, his jocular tone. But he dispelled the thought, chalking his distrust up to his habitual distrust of everything. How, he wondered, would he expect this Kurtz to act, anyway?

Calder let the door close gently as they entered the stairwell.

Upstairs, Pollack again glanced at his watch and again cursed his lack of control. The numbers of reporters jostling to get into the White House had grown. Cameramen were the most egregious pushers. The way they hoisted the cameras over their heads reminded him of crabs in a pot, each climbing over the other to get out. Pollack was grateful for the relative calm of his position. The hallway was empty, as he had requested, but he was getting nervous about trying to make it through the crowd once Imogen and the professor arrived. He glanced again at his watch. "Come on, come on," he whispered.

"There's a slight change in plan," said Kurtz. "Something Pollack doesn't know yet. We were going to go out of the building and cross Executive Avenue and come in through the White House west gate, but there are far too many people around. Too hard to control, too many variables. We'll go up to the first level to get Pollack—he's waiting there for us— then come back down to level two. I made sure it was clear . . . that is, safe . . . and walk across the garage to the North stairwell, which lets us right onto the tunnel and into the White House. Got it?" Kurtz turned to look behind him.

Not knowing the territory, they could only agree. Kurtz smiled again.

"This isn't the way I'd have liked to have done it," he continued. He looked ruefully at Imogen. "I'm not sure I like all this secrecy, but I guess it's the way you wanted it." The three continued up the stairs, Calder bringing up the rear.

"So what's the plan?" asked Kurtz. "What do you two think is going on?"

Before Imogen could answer, Kurtz held up a hand.

At each landing, Kurtz would pause briefly and look up before continuing. Imogen felt herself becoming calmer with each level closer to the air. She didn't like Kurtz being involved, but acknowledged to herself that it had probably been necessary and that Pollack's including him was natural.

As Kurtz glanced upward at each landing, Calder glanced down. "Don't worry professor," Kurtz assured him, "I've been thorough. It's going to be dicey getting through security in the tunnel, but we'll manage if you let me and Pollack do the talking. I don't want to have to explain more than is necessary. Neither of you is armed, right?"

"No," said Calder.

"And your gun is still at your apartment, Gen. Right?"

Imogen paused. Kurtz stopped a moment, paused before turning around. "Am I right?" he asked.

"Yes . . . it—"

"—I remember where you keep it, Gen. I didn't imagine you had time to get it."

"No. You're right. I didn't." Imogen shrugged off the little warning voice in the back of her mind. Of course Kurtz knew where she kept her gun, she said to herself. He'd been in the apartment enough. Of course he would ask if we were armed under these circumstances.

"Almost there," said Kurtz brightly. "This is the level we will use to cross to the other stairwell. You two wait here. I'm just going up to get Pollack and then we'll all go across."

Imogen and Duncan waited on the landing. As Kurtz pushed open the door above them, a shaft of light from the flood lights outside filled the stairwell. A moment later, the silhouette of Pollack eclipsed the light.

"Doug," said Kurtz as they walked down to Calder and Imogen, "I think we should use the tunnel. I don't like all those reporters. We'd have to walk right through them to get in."

"I agree," said Pollack. Extending his hand, he said "Imogen. Professor—"

"Everything's in hand, Genny," said Pollack. "I just hope you two can help us fix this mess." As he gave them each a pass, Kurtz pushed past. "As soon as we get in the tunnel, you need to tell me everything."

"All right," Kurtz said, "My lead."

Pollack and Calder felt grateful for Kurtz's gruff assertiveness. Calder particularly welcomed the feeling of finally getting things done. Imogen hung back slightly, irked at Kurtz.

"We go through here and across," Kurtz was saying, "and straight across the parking garage. It's empty, but I still don't like it. I'll lead."

"What don't you like, Tom?" asked Pollack as they rounded the second landing.

"Just being cautious. I wish we had more agents. And with seven dead Electors on our hands, I don't much like the prospect of any more when these are the only two who know what's going on."

Imogen felt a crack of adrenaline, the warning that sounds before the reason for it can be articulated. Kurtz opened the door to the deserted level two and walked through, pausing just long enough for Pollack to catch the door and hold it open. How did Kurtz know how many dead Electors there had been? she wondered.

Imogen was two steps from the landing when she quickened her pace and caught the heavy door: "Duncan!" she whispered harshly. As she did so, Kurtz wheeled around, his gun drawn. The silenced shot, aimed at Pollack, found its mark below his left shoulder. Pollack's upper body twisted and spun with the force of the bullet's impact, his chest erupting in blood. Calder took a step backwards and turned to run back through the door.

Kurtz dropped the gun and withdrew his service weapon. He fired, catching Calder in the right shoulder blade. The shot echoed deafeningly in the empty garage. Calder fell forward through the doorway onto his hands and knees. Imogen flung the door closed. A second shot ricocheted off the door as it slammed shut.

Imogen bent down to help Calder up. "Run!" he shouted. She stepped over him and began sprinting up the stairs, Calder stumbling after her as best he could. Below, she heard the door to the second level blast open. Kurtz fired again at Calder, grazing his ribs under his right armpit. Calder cried out but she heard him still moving.

After a few more steps, Calder fell onto the stairs, slipping in his own blood. Imogen, still running, looked down over the railing. Kurtz was poised. He fired, narrowly missing her. Imogen recoiled against the far wall as the bullet sang against the metal.

As she paused, wondering whether it was safe to continue up, the sound of gunfire resounded in her ears, like a tuning fork against the skull. Fear gripped her more tightly than she had ever known. Then another shot, this one nowhere near her, and she began to climb again.

Half a flight below, with Kurtz's attention on Imogen, Calder bounded over the bend in the stairs and rushed at Kurtz as he stood peering up the stairs. Calder drove into Kurtz as he had the assassin in the hallway. Kurtz was nimbler and slipped out of the way just as Calder was about to slam into him. Calder crashed into the wall as Kurtz twisted to fire and missed. Calder wheeled and closed on Kurtz before he could fire again, grabbing at his shooting hand.

Kurtz slammed his forehead across the bridge of Calder's nose. The pain and shock sent Calder reeling into the adjacent wall. Kurtz stepped back, steadied himself and lifted his gun. As he did so, the second floor door burst open, and Pollack fired four shots into Kurtz. Kurtz fell backward onto the stairs, dead.

"Genny?" asked Pollack, leaning against the door frame, blood covering his front.

Calder, unable to speak, nodded and pointed upward.

"Genny!" Pollack called. "Kurtz is dead. Come this way. Hurry."

Calder lost his battle with gravity and slid sideways down the wall, as Imogen sprinted down the steps. She gasped as she saw the carnage at the bottom of the stairs.

Pollack, on one knee, now fell heavily against the doorframe. He pulled a radio from his belt. "Emergency clear," he said somewhat breathlessly into the radio. "This is Pollack, FBI, for agent Bennett."

"Bennett," came the immediate reply. "What is the

nature—"

"—Shots fired, level two parking garage, Old Exec Building. Threat neutralized. Respond to me at Stair W2."

Imogen stepped off the last step onto the landing and walked toward Calder. There was so much blood everywhere. Calder was sinking against the wall. She reached out to touch his face. Calder smiled weakly and closed his eyes, his cheek settling into her hand.

From across the empty garage, four agents in full body armor fanned out from the east door. The first three stopped in the middle of the lot, and fell to one knee, each taking up a strategic position. Each aimed his machine gun at a threat point—one at the north stairwell door, one at them in the west stair and one south, toward the car ramp. A moment later, as the first agents took up their positions, another agent sprinted out from the door. He stopped, turned, and trained his gun on the door they had all just come through. The last of the four agents to emerge said something into his headset, and two more agents, these two in business suits, appeared at the door and ran past the four on the ground toward Pollack, their guns drawn, aimed at Pollack.

The first agent arrived at the west stair doorway and fell to one knee. His partner remained four paces behind, his gun drawn and trained on the three in the stairwell.

"Agent Pollack," said the first agent on the scene glancing quickly but carefully at the identity card Pollack proffered, "you're injured."

"Yes," said Pollack, breathing unevenly.

Behind the first agent, his partner holstered his gun and began giving crisp orders into the microphone in his sleeve.

"Take Agent Trager here to the Attorney General," said Pollack. "That is the objective. No one else. Your responsibility."

"Agent Trager," he said, holding out his hand. Then, over his shoulder, "Steele, Immermann, with me. Larew," he said to the agent at his side, "your site."

Larew was already working: "This is agent Larew. Three med-evac to stairwell W-2," he said into the radio. "Get Crime Scene down here, too."

The first agent led Imogen a few paces away from the carnage and stopped. He examined Imogen's pass, her ID. Immermann quickly frisked her. Satisfied, the agent said "Let's go." He led, Imogen following behind, Steele and Immermann falling in behind to the right and left of her.

"Two med-evac," Pollack corrected, speaking to Larew. "One for me. One for Calder there." He looked over at the lifeless body of Kurtz, twisted and bloody.

"Is that Agent Kurtz?" Larew asked staring toward the body.

"Yeah," said Pollack, and thought 'fuck him'!

Calder's eyes were closing now. He felt warm, peaceful. He liked the quiet.

Imogen and the Secret Service agents went out through the North exit. The door slammed shut. Pollack felt sick with dread as heard the door close. He hoped that he hadn't just sent Imogen to her death. He fumbled for his phone, opened Imogen's email and forwarded it to Callahan at the *Washington Post*.

ELECTION

An hour later, Imogen found herself standing next to the Attorney General at the press conference, giving a summary of what she knew to the assembled reporters. She read off the names of the murdered Electors, the names of Matthew Yamashita who had found the evidence and Jerry Ingram, who had died while digging into it. She paused, hoping desperately that Pollack's and Calder's names would not be added to the list. The Attorney General announced that the Department of Justice had opened investigations into each of the seven Elector deaths. Further, as material witnesses, the three Faithless Electors were to be brought into protective custody immediately.

The president for his part, urged calm, and together with the newly designated president-elect, he asked the nation to allow the Department of Justice to do its investigation before leaping wildly to conclusions.

"A chaotic, bitterly fought primary season," he said, "has begot a rancorous, cynical, illegally fought campaign. The nation now needs to come together and rally around this issue." The president felt sure that far from exposing a weakness, "the following weeks would be this nation's finest hour, and it will make us stronger."

But the three Faithless Electors were not taken into custody. Although the Attorney General had given the order to detain them moments before going in front of the reporters, each had been executed before the press conference was over.

In the following days, the FBI found that much of the evidence and notes surrounding the original seven murdered Electors—originally designated accidents—were missing from files at various local police stations and sheriff's offices. Kurtz had been the only known insider, and he was dead, too. The FBI continued looking into his background, movements, his cell and email history, but they had yet to find any clues.

Calder and Pollack survived their wounds, but were oblivious to the convulsions of the nation. Each had been rushed to Fort Belvoir Hospital in Virginia where they received transfusions, operations and reconstructive surgeries--Pollack for his shattered left shoulder and clavicle, Calder for his right shoulder.

The first week for both had been spent flitting in and out of consciousness, waking to the faces of concerned doctors and impatient interrogators. The second week, they were each growing stronger but were easily tired by questioning. Both felt they would do better recuperating at home, but Justice wanted to keep a sharp eye on both. Pollack was in hot water for having forwarded Imogen's email to the press. His assertion that his action had been prudent in the face of a clear conspiracy involving even a Special Agent and the possibility of other agency infiltration was met with blank disdain.

In the third week, on Friday, January 6, 2017, at 1 p.m. the new congress met to certify the Electoral College Vote. Calder and Pollack were still being held at Fort Belvoir "for observation." They met in their hospital wing's empty lounge to watch on television as the 115th Congress began. Calder noticed the multiple camera nodes in the ceiling throughout the lounge and assumed there were equally miniature microphones secreted everywhere. He felt as much "on stage" as the Congressmen.

The new Speaker having been duly elected by the majority party, the House turned to the election of the president. The Speaker announced the result, 270 for James Christopher and 268 for Diane Redmond. The leader of the Opposition made a motion that the three switched Electoral votes be declared invalid due to fraud. The motion to declare the three votes invalid was seconded. The House voted, and all voted to declare the three invalid.

"So far, so good," said Pollack.

The Speaker conferred a moment with staff and council and then announced that "No candidate having the necessary clear majority of Electoral votes, the House will use the constitutional procedure whereby each state has one vote, as is provided in Article Two." As this procedure would require state caucuses, the speaker announced an adjournment until the next day.

"So, what do you think, Professor?" asked Pollack. "Tomorrow all the states vote for the actual Electoral College Vote winner—fifty to zero?"

Calder stared at the screen, wondering how many ballots there would be over the next days before there was a winner. "Heart-warming," he said. "But improbable."

In Wichita, two other men also sat watching the national broadcast. "Well, that really is it," said one. "We tried. It's over."

His compatriot rose from his chair and picked up the phone. "The hell it is!"

James McCrone graduated in 1990 from the University of Washington in Seattle with a Master of Fine Arts degree in Creative Writing.

He currently resides in Oxford, UK, but will be returning to the United States in the summer of 2016. *Faithless Elector* is his first published novel.

Look for more in this series, including *Dark Network,* coming soon.

CPSIA information can be obtained
at www.ICGtesting.com
Printed in the USA
LVOW12s1045040916

503165LV00001B/192/P